Please return/renew this item
by the last date shown.
Books can also be renewed at
www.bolton.gov.uk/libraries

The Road Agent

What should have been the simple robbery of a stagecoach for outlaw Brent Clancy turns into a deadly game of wits with a band of assassins determined to kill the President of the United States. In the course of this adventure, the one-time road agent finds himself on the right side of the law for a novelty, fighting both to save the president's life while at the same time avenging a personal grievance.

The Road
Agent

Clyde Barker

A Black Horse Western

ROBERT HALE

© Clyde Barker 2018
First published in Great Britain 2018
Paperback edition 2019

ISBN 978-0-7198-3019-8

The Crowood Press
The Stable Block
Crowood Lane
Ramsbury
Marlborough
Wiltshire SN8 2HR

www.bhwesterns.com

Robert Hale is an imprint
of The Crowood Press

Typeset by Derek Doyle & Associates, Shaw Heath
Printed and bound in Great Britain by
4Bind Ltd, Stevenage, SG1 2XT

CHAPTER 1

The mule was labouring sullenly under its load, which consisted of two glass carboys, each containing five gallons of oily, grey sludge. These bulbous bottles, encased in raffia and straw, were slung over the beast's back, one hanging on either side. Two men walked along with the mule. Both seemed excessively attentive to the animal; constantly reaching out anxious hands to steady it, if it appeared to be faltering or about to stumble. This solicitousness was motivated less by any tender regard for the welfare of a dumb animal than by their own instincts of self-preservation. The fact was that the mule was carrying on its back eighty pounds of nitroglycerine, which was more than enough to blow them all to smithereens if the tired creature should happen to miss its footing.

'I don't reckon that this here is the best means to go about this business,' said the younger of the two men, who looked to be about thirty years of age. 'From all I am able to collect, this stuff will go off if

5

anybody so much as farts near it. What if this creature falls down?' His companion, who was older, plumper and more jovial, looked at him quizzically.

'Scared, are you? I am surprised, I heard tell that you rebels were game for anything.'

The young man looked at him coldly. 'Rebel, is it? I tell you now, I'm game for anything in the fighting and killing line, but this is another matter. I don't see where we have to carry this here along this track in this way. Like I say, that creature stumbles and we are both done for.'

The older man said nothing for a spell. Then he remarked, 'It's how your boss would have it. He wants to know that the nitro will accomplish the job he has in mind. He wants further to be sure of the quantity needed and such like. I am being paid for this. If I am not worried, I can't see what it should be to you.'

The two men and the mule trudged on for another half an hour without speaking again until they came into view of an old mission station. It had been built near a fort that no longer existed and had been abandoned during the war. A substantial and robust building, it was fashioned partly of stone and partly of wood and adobe.

When the party arrived at the old building, the men very carefully lifted the carboys from the mule's back and set them against the wall of the mission. Having done this, the two of them had a bite to eat and smoked a little. The older man had forbidden any smoking while they were actually engaged in transporting the explosives.

After they had rested, the younger man took a sketchpad out of his knapsack and drew the building in front of them. He then paced out the measurements of the place and made notes about its construction. When he had finished, there was a pretty detailed account of the size and nature of the structure near to which almost a hundred pounds of high explosive was about to be detonated. Having done all this, he went back to where he had left his rifle. It was a seven-shot Spencer carbine and it could be sighted up to eight hundred yards. After it had been loaded and he had checked too the old navy Colt tucked in his belt, the two of them, with the mule plodding along behind, made for a rise of ground that lay the better part of half a mile or so from the mission station. The young man led them to the crest, where he stopped. He turned to the other and asked, 'You think this is far enough for us to be safe?'

The other man shrugged. 'I should say so. You want to be close enough to see the result, don't you? I thought your people wanted an account from you of the damage wrought?'

The man with the rifle lay down in the dust and placed the stock of the rifle to his shoulder. He squinted at the target. At half a mile, he could just catch the glint of glass in the sunlight and he was confident that the Spencer would not let him down. It never had yet. 'You going to lay down?' he enquired. The older man shook his head contemptuously.

The shot from the rifle was deafening so close up, but it was as nothing to the roar of sound that struck them both a fraction of a second later. The ground shook and a gust of warm air blew past them, stirring up the dirt. Then, a steady rain of chips of stone, fragments of wood and chunks of plaster began to fall on and around them. The mule brayed in alarm. The mission station itself had disappeared behind a cloud of smoke and dust.

'God almighty,' observed the young man, awestruck, 'I seed some explosions in the war, but never one to match this. One time, a magazine of powder went up, but it was nothing to this.'

As the smoke cleared, they could see that the stout building had all but vanished. The walls had been reduced to around three or four feet in height and they encircled an empty space. The whole place had been blown to pieces and those pieces scattered far and wide. The two men walked down the slope to inspect the ruins.

'Well, that powerful enough for you and your friends?' asked the older man. 'I tell you now, that Black Hercules is like nothing on Earth. It is twice the strength of ordinary nitro.'

'Yeah, I reckon that is just what we need. By my reckoning, that stuff should leave no survivors or nothing standing.' The former Confederate soldier turned to face his companion. They stood ten feet or so apart. 'Only thing is, you see, we don't plan to buy from you. We have found a man who will make it for us on the spot. Still and all, I thank you for giving the

8

demonstration. You may be sure that I will tell my boss that this is the goods for the job.'

'You needn't take that line, my friend. You try to cut me out now and see what happens to your precious secret.'

The other man laughed. 'I thought you might say so.' He drew his pistol, cocking it with his thumb as he did so. 'Remind me, what was it you said to me back on the road, you Yankee bastard? Something about 'scared' and 'rebels' wasn't it?'

'You wouldn't shoot down an unarmed man. Where is your honour?'

The ball took him in the chest and he put his hand to the wound wonderingly, unable to believe what had happened. The second ball caught him right smack on the forehead, whereupon he dropped lifeless to the ground.

After examining the scene of the explosion carefully and making some more sketches and notes, the young man jumped onto the mule and the two of them made their way back to town.

When, after four years of the bloodiest slaughter ever known to man, the great War Between the States drew to a close in 1865, most of the men who had fought in that conflict desired nothing more than to return to peaceful and productive lives. Some though, a small but significant minority, had acquired a taste for hazard and adventure that could not be sated by working on railroads or ranches; nor by clerking in stores, toiling in offices or digging ditches either. These men, most of them young enough to have spent the early years of their manhood in the Union or Confederate armed forces, found themselves wholly unable to settle down after the war ended. Some re-enlisted and took part in the Indian Wars, while others became lawmen. Then again, there were those who turned bad and took to robbery and rapine to provide them with the feeling of danger and sense of excitement to which they had somehow become addicted during the late war. One such individual was Brent Clancy.

At the age of sixteen, Brent Clancy had lied about his age and joined the Union army, following Mr Lincoln's appeal for volunteers in April 1861. He had then served right the way through the war, ending up at Appomattox Court House precisely four years later, on 9 April 1865, the day that the instrument of surrender was signed by General Lee. When he left the army, later that year, Clancy found that he could not settle to one thing or live in any particular place for more than a few weeks, or a month or two at most. He was fiddle-footed and restless and had to keep on the move. He also needed the thrill of pitting his wits against others in a life or death struggle for survival.

So it was that a sunny summer's day in 1866 found Brent Clancy seated on his horse and waiting on a rise of land overlooking the dirt track running between two little towns, one of which was in Kansas and the other Missouri. The stage was due any time now and it was Clancy's intention to rob the passengers of anything they might possess in the way of watches, jewellery or cash-money. He had chosen this part of the route because it was, as far as anybody was able to gauge, just precisely on the border between the states of Kansas and Missouri. Clancy's choice of this spot to spring his ambush was by no means fortuitous. He had found that if some fairly trifling crime took place on the edge of one jurisdiction, then sometimes the local law would purport to believe that the offence had been committed on the other side of the state line and so decline to investigate, hoping that somebody else would handle the matter. If the sheriff on the other side of the line adopted a similar approach, then there was an excellent chance of this disputed jurisdiction leading to nobody being minded strongly enough to start pursuing the man responsible. Of course, this didn't happen if some serious felony such as murder or rape was involved, but Brent Clancy took great care not to be mixed up in such affairs.

Among those who were, like he himself, on the scout, Clancy would own to being a road agent. This was a facetious term for those who preyed upon stagecoaches and lone riders; similar in many ways to the highwaymen who once infested the roads of old-time England. Sometimes such men operated in teams. Others, like Clancy, preferred to work alone. The returns on this form of robbery were not high and such enterprises were not without risk; but it suited Brent Clancy well enough. He did not target consignments of bullion, which might be more heavily guarded than the usual passenger runs, nor had he yet harmed anybody. His activities so far had been bloodless and conducted with as much good humour as was possible when one man is robbing others.

In the distance, the stage hove into view and Clancy's sharp eyes at once discerned that there was only one man driving it. Nobody was riding shotgun. This was apt to make the whole enterprise far more agreeable and reduced the risk of a gun battle, which was the last thing Brent Clancy was looking for. As the stage rattled its way along, it was now about a half-mile away, he pulled up his neckerchief and adjusted it over the lower half of his face in approved bandit fashion. Then he rode down the slope to intercept the scarlet coach and relieve its occupants of anything that he might find useful.

Once Clancy had reached the bottom of the slope and was on the track itself he withdrew from a scabbard hanging in front of his saddle, a sawn-off scattergun. So short was the barrel of this piece that its load of nuts, screws, buckshot and scraps of metal would fan out and catch anybody within a radius of about twenty feet. It was no manner of use for hitting any particular target, but for spreading injury and death over a wide area, there was no better weapon. The fellow in charge of the team of horses pulling the stage evidently had no inclination to risk falling foul of Brent Clancy's shotgun, for he reined in as the young man trotted his horse forward, applying the brakes as he did so and then, so there could be no possible misapprehension as touching upon his own pacific intentions, he raised both hands above his head as well.

The driver of the stagecoach was a man in his riper years, with sparse grey hair and a deeply lined countenance. He said in a resigned voice, 'Well young man, what will you have?'

'Just climb down from your perch there and invite your passengers to step out where I can see them. You might apprise 'em of the fact that I'm ready to shoot any man, woman or child as shows defiance, while you're about it.'

The man in charge of the stage apparently had a fund of common sense, coupled with a strong instinct for survival, for he clambered down without another word and, walking over to the door of the coach, called through the open window. 'Don't none o' you folks fret now, but we're a being robbed. Just do as this young villain tells you and we should come out the situation with our lives. He's bearing down on me this minute with a scattergun, so nobody do anything sudden or unexpected. You all come on out now.'

Upon these hints, the four passengers emerged blinking into the sunlight and Clancy saw to his dismay that one of them was known to him. This was a young girl, scarcely old enough to have started putting up her hair, whom he had met at a hurdy house in the Kansas town of Sheridan. Clancy had visited the hurdy-gurdy house for three nights running, the previous week, flirting with and striking up something of a friendship with Maggie. It had amounted to no more than a little canoodling, nothing serious, but the girl would surely remember him, even with his mouth and nose concealed in this way. So it proved, for as soon as she stepped down from the coach and glanced up at the rider who was menacing them, Maggie had squealed girlishly and cried, 'Oooh, Clancy!'

Brent Clancy's eyes blazed at the hapless young woman and she realized that she had put a foot wrong, saying hurriedly, 'Oh, beg pardon, I took you for another.'

The three other people from the coach, all men, stood around trying to look as though they were tough, but somehow didn't feel that day like tackling this young robber. Two of them were respectable-looking young men, a little older than Clancy himself. The third was a swarthy fellow of about forty-five or fifty, who was immaculately turned out and looked as though he were not in the habit of mixing with common folk, unless he could help it. None of the three men were carrying guns; at least as far as Clancy could see. He dismounted, all the while keeping an eye on the others, for fear of treachery. When he was on firm ground, he said, 'I'll thank you all to place your wallets, watches and suchlike on the ground in a pile. If nobody fools around, then there'll be no bloodshed today, leastways, not on my account.'

The younger men slowly removed billfolds and

set them carefully on the ground. One of them had also a watch; an expensive-looking gold hunter. This, he disengaged from his vest pocket and, with every show of the greatest reluctance, set it down beside the two wallets. The older man took a little longer. He was handicapped by having in one hand a morocco-bound vanity case, the kind of thing that might contain shaving tackle. He had to shift this from one hand to another, in order to take out his watch and then fumble in his pockets for his money. Brent Clancy observed him shrewdly, noting that he seemed excessively anxious not to be separated from his little case for a single second. This was enough to persuade Clancy that here was something valuable. He said to the man, 'Just lay that case down there as well, along with the rest of the stuff.'

'It is nothing in here, nothing but a few papers. They're private matters, not worth a cent to you.'

'Well,' said Brent Clancy, 'I reckon as I'll be the best judge o' that. Just you set it down there.'

But the fellow was obdurate and stubborn as a mule and held onto the little case as though his very life depended upon it. He shook his head, saying, 'You'll not be having this.'

Now the one thing needful if you're wanting to be robbing a bunch of folk is to show that you mean business and will stick at nothing. If once there is any suggestion of weakness or lack of resolve, then before you know it, your erstwhile victims will be banding together to turn the tables and overpower you. Clancy knew of instances where this had happened and the failed robber had been beaten to death by enraged citizens or, in one awful case, subdued and then strung up from a nearby tree. He did not propose to fall prey to any mishap of this nature and so strode forward and grabbed at the leather-bound article in question. The man holding it gripped all the tighter and as he tugged at it, Clancy was aware out of the corner of his eye of the other two male passengers making as though to move forward.

Unless he acted swiftly, Clancy knew that things would soon spiral out of his control and so he released hold of the contested article, stepped back a pace and then reversed the scattergun and slammed the stock as hard as he could against the skull of the man with whom he had been disputing. The results far exceeded his expectations, for the simple reason that he had momentarily forgotten that he had cocked both barrels of the thing before commencing operations. The consequence was that one of the hammers came down and one barrel of the scattergun fired up into the sky.

The roar of the shot echoed across the grassy plain like thunder, causing the passengers to leap back in alarm and wonder if their last moments had arrived. Clancy, who had felt a searing pain in his cheek as the weapon went off, twisted the scattergun so that he was once again holding it by the stock and covering the others. Holding the gun at his hip, he raised his left hand to his face and was less than enchanted to discover that he was all over blood. A fragment of the scrap metal must have gouged a furrow along his cheek. He said irritably, 'You all satisfied now? I'm more'n half minded to shoot somebody down this minute. I damned near lost an eye there!' He stooped down and picked up the little morocco-bound case which had caused the trouble. Its owner lay on the ground stunned.

The unplanned shooting had certainly driven all thoughts of resistance from those that Clancy was robbing. He presented, had he but known it, a ghastly sight. His eyes were wild and blood was running freely down his cheek and dripping from his chin. Nobody felt minded to tackle him now. Even little Maggie looked scared and was gazing in terror at the man whom she had previously thought of as a charming and good-humoured sort. It struck Clancy that this poor thing was actually afraid of him.

Maggie was wearing a pair of gold earbobs; embellished with seed-pearls. She had told him that these had been left her by her grandmama. He wasn't such a dog as to deprive her of a treasured heirloom, but thought it incumbent upon him to offer some explanation to his other victims as to why he was excluding the girl from his depredations. If he appeared to favour her in any way, some fool would next be accusing her of being his accomplice and it could go ill with her. He said, 'I'll warrant all your gee-gaws are naught but pinchbeck, miss. They're no use to me. You have any cash-money about your person?'

'Not a cent,' said the girl frankly, 'I'm being met at

the other end by somebody.'

Brent Clancy looked over the passengers and driver and said, 'You folk take yourself off aways, just walk a hundred yards over yonder. Then I'll leave you all be.'

Sullenly, with a few murmurs of discontent, the men walked off in the direction that Clancy had indicated with a wave of his hand. Before she left, he caught Maggie's eye and gave her an almost imperceptible wink, which she acknowledged with the merest nod of her head. The only one who marked this brief exchange was the man whose case had been wrested from him by main force. He gave no outward indication of having noticed anything amiss, but was satisfied in his own mind that the young girl with whom he had been travelling could, at the very least, set him on the trail of the man who had stolen his property.

Once everybody was clear out of the way, Brent Clancy scooped up the loot and stowed it in his saddle-bag. Then he shook the dust of that place from his feet, mounted his horse and, urging on the mare, set off at a canter, aiming to put as much distance as he could between himself and the site of his latest crime.

On a Friday night, eight months before Clancy had knocked over the stage running between Missouri and Kansas, nine men met in a room on the first floor of a saloon in Pulaski, Tennessee. It lacked just three days to Christmas. Legend would later have it that only six men were present at the meeting and that it took place on the very night before Christmas, but this was not so. The names of six of the men are well known. They were John C. Lester, John B. Kennedy, James R. Crowe, Frank Mason, Richard R. Reed, and J. Calvin Jones, and their purpose in gathering that night was to found the organisation that was to become known as the Ku Klux Klan. What is not generally known is that former Confederate generals Nathan Bedford Forrest, George Gordon and Patrick Abernathy Mason were also there that night. While the crowd downstairs in the saloon were getting liquored up, the three generals outlined an audacious plan; a scheme that, it was hoped, would change the course of history.

Following the Confederate surrender in April, which had brought the civil war to an end, there had been an uneasy peace throughout the south. Now, seven months later, after realizing that their states would be under military rule for years to come, many of the thousands of demobilised soldiers had licked their wounds and were ready again to fight against the Federal Government in defence of states' rights. The Southern Cause had suffered a serious setback, but it was far from finished. The purpose of the meeting that night was to harness the simmering discontent felt by so many in the South and use it to help the Confederacy rise from the ashes of its ruin.

History has judged the Ku Klux Klan harshly, dismissing it as little better than a gang of hooligans whose aim was to terrorise the newly freed black slaves. This was, as far as it goes, perfectly true. Every member of the organisation in the years that followed that first meeting in Pulaski swore a solemn oath devised by former Brigadier-General Gordon, that they believed in 'a white man's government and the emancipation of the white men of the South and the restitution of the Southern people of all their rights'. In short, the aim was the restoration of the Confederacy and the renewed subjugation of the former slaves.

The nine men meeting in that room talked long into the night about the means by which Southern Rights were to be regained. The generals outlined their strategy, which was a subtle and cunning one. On the one hand, the new organisation would work on a local level to keep down blacks who were inclined to get a little uppity, what with all the 'freedom' they were being promised. This end was to be achieved by the judicious use of beatings, lynching and the burning of homes. At the same time, the Ku Klux Klan would be forged into what amounted to a secret army; a force hundreds of thousands strong who would be ready to wrest control of the South from the Yankee invaders, just as soon as the time was ripe. This would entail biding their time for at least another nine months or so.

It was then, after they had been talking for three hours or more, that General Forrest revealed the final piece of the plan; the culmination of all their plotting. He dressed the matter up in various fancy metaphors, talking of 'cutting off the snake's head' and suchlike, but the gist of the thing was clear. In the high summer of the following year, 1866, the key figures of the Federal Government would be removed. The president, secretary of state and a number of generals would all be cut down as though by a bolt of lightning. The nation would be left rudderless and this was to be the signal for a general rising in the South, which would be accompanied by the simultaneous assassination of Republican politicians, carpetbaggers, scalawags and all the other figures who looked set to make life a misery in the South for the foreseeable future.

General Forrest would not be drawn on the method by which the wholesale removal of the leading figures of the Federal Government might be achieved. Nor would he explain how the Yankee army would be prevented from wreaking revenge upon the South. He limited himself to observing that 'Those Yankees heard our "rebel yell" often enough in the war, gentlemen. I tell you now, the rebel yell they will hear next, will be the loudest ever. I venture to suggest that this enterprise, which we are calling "Operation Rebel Yell", will not only restore the South to its rightful position, but will sound the death knell for the Union itself.'

CHAPTER 2

There was some exceedingly lively and animated conversation in the stagecoach that Clancy had held up as it proceeded on its way to the Missouri town of Indian Falls. The general thrust of the conversation was between the two younger men, who would, it seems, have made short work of the road agent who had interrupted their journey were it not for their fears about a young lady being exposed to violence or some other species of unpleasantness. If not for this consideration, the theme of their angry declarations was that there were no lengths to which they would not have gone in tackling that desperado.

The two other passengers in the stage were singularly unimpressed by the braggadocio of the youngsters. Maggie stared moodily out of the window, thinking wistfully of the time that she had spent with Clancy, while the older man eyed the youngsters with undisguised contempt. He was the only one who had resisted and had had his head cut open in the process.

Frank Mason had been one of those present when the Klan was founded and what those involved referred to as the 'Great Enterprise' was launched. He had been carrying various documents and notes relating to both matters in a vanity case and that they had now fallen into the hands of some wild young bushwhacker was little short of a disaster. It was not so much that the information contained in the little case was irreplaceable; more that in the wrong hands there was enough there to alert Washington to what was afoot, which could in turn spike the guns of the conspirators in no small measure. It was of the utmost importance to recover the papers before any mischief resulted from their loss and also to silence the boy who had made off with them. True, the information was for the most part in cypher, but so weighty was the matter that no chances could be taken. Any cypher can be broken in time.

That the young rascal who had robbed him was evidently known to the girl sitting at his side had not escaped Frank Mason's notice. He had both heard her startled exclamation when first she laid eyes on the robber and also observed the slight wink which he had given her as they parted. Mason would take oath that the two of them were somehow connected, which meant in turn that he must stick closer than a cocklebur to the young woman and try to get her alone when they arrived at their destination.

Maggie Hardcastle had not a cent to her name and was relying upon a mutual acquaintance meeting her when she reached town and taking care of her until she was settled in her new position, which was another hurdy-gurdy house in Indian Falls. Hurdy houses were a little different from ordinary saloons. They provided men with not only food and liquor, but also the opportunity to get to know young women who were apt to be a little more free and easy with their favours than was generally the case with respectable girls. Music was provided by a man with a hurdy-gurdy and those who wished could dance and get to hold some girl a little closer than was conventional. The girls themselves wore skirts short enough to reveal their knees, which was a scandalous thing to many upright citizens and accounted for the stiff opposition in some towns to the opening of a hurdy house. The rumour was that many of the young women employed in such places were willing, for sufficient monetary compensation, to go a deal further than merely dancing with customers. In fact, it was sometimes suggested, such places were little better than cat-houses.

The hurdy-gurdy house at which Maggie had been working in Sheridan was indeed as much a brothel as it was somewhere to drink and dance, and this had led to her leaving, or rather being asked to leave, the place. Maggie Hardcastle did not mind exposing her legs a little, nor to flirting and canoodling with some of the men who frequented the Sheridan house. She drew the line, however, at anything more than that and refused flatly to go upstairs with any of the customers, in order, as she put it, to go the whole hog. The manager had intimated to her that if she continued in this way, then their paths would have to part. As he had reasoned the matter out to her forty-eight hours earlier, 'Strikes me girl, you're a mite too delicate for this line o' work! Happen you'd do better teaching in Sunday school or something of that kind. The boys we get here want something more than a kiss and a cuddle in the corner of the barroom, if you take my meaning.'

Having already come to much the same conclusion as the manager of the hurdy house, Maggie had promptly arranged to leave. She had sent word the previous week to a friend of hers in Indian Falls, asking if she would meet her from the stage in a se'n night. Thus it was that when the stagecoach drew in to Indian Falls and she disembarked, Maggie looked round eagerly for Josephine, her friend. Josephine, however, was nowhere to be seen and Maggie found herself in the disagreeable position of being in an unknown town that she had never before visited. With growing despair, she realized that she could not recollect her friend's address either. She had been depending upon being met when she got here.

As Maggie stood, looking helplessly and forlornly around her, somebody tapped her gently on the shoulder. Turning, she saw that it was the older man who had been sitting next to her during the journey. He said diffidently, as though shy of his intentions being mistaken, 'I hope I ain't troubling you miss, but you look a little lost. Is there aught that I can do, to be of service?'

Although he looked closer to fifty than forty, the man was good-looking and had a courtly manner. Maggie said, 'I was supposed to be meeting somebody here, but the party hasn't shown up.'

'Well, if I'm not being too forward, might I offer to buy you some refreshments, while we think what is to be done? I hate to see a lady in difficulties.'

Had the man been a few years younger, Maggie Hardcastle would have politely, but firmly, declined the offer of help. However, this fellow looked old enough to be her father and had a pleasant way with him; like an uncle or something. He spoke too with an educated voice, which further served to make him appear trustworthy. She said, 'Well, that's right kind of you, sir. My name's Maggie. Maggie Hardcastle.'

Bowing courteously, the man said, 'And I am Nathaniel Delaney, Miss Hardcastle, and I am delighted to make your acquaintance. I am entirely at your disposal.'

Brent Clancy was not in the best of humours as he rode east, heading into Missouri. The wound to his cheek was a shallow one, but had nevertheless bled profusely. Apart from the attention that such a mark on his face might bring, just at the very time that he hoped to travel along without being the object of anybody's remark, there was too the matter of his vanity. He prided himself on his good looks and the idea of having a scar down the side of his face irked him. Still, there it was, thought Clancy. A way of life such as this was bound to end in the occasional shot being fired.

After holding up the stage, Clancy had been left with a choice. He could hardly head back to Sheridan or on to Indian Falls. News of the robbery would spread soon enough and the sudden appearance of a wanderer with blood on his face would be likely to attract questions. He wished to get altogether away from the stagecoach route that ran from east to west and so he really had to decide if he would be going north or south. North would take him into more civilised parts; places like Kansas City or Topeka, both of which had well-organised and efficient police forces and good local law enforcement, which was not at all what Clancy was seeking! South, on the other hand, was Arkansas on one side and the Indian nations on the other. Both were a little wilder and less civilised than some parts of the country and so it was a natural choice that he should head in that general direction. He recalled talking over his possible destinations with Maggie, for she had been on the point of moving on herself and did not appear to know this part of the country too well.

It was while he was weighing up the advantages of one destination over another that Clancy became aware that he was being trailed by two men who were, like him, on horseback. He had a sixth sense for danger and had it not been for this, Clancy might have dismissed the pair as no more than travellers who chanced to be going in the same direction as he himself. They were a half mile behind, but from what he could see, the two of them were moving faster than he and would catch up with him by and by. He had no especial reason to suppose that these other travellers meant him any harm, but Brent Clancy had not survived through the whole of the war by taking things for granted and being careless of his security. It was by always treating strangers as potential enemies that he had made it safely past his twenty-first birthday.

The track along which he was riding led through a featureless sea of grassland, but ahead lay a little wooded valley, which suggested to Clancy some opportunity for concealment. At the very least, it might afford him a chance to surprise those coming up from behind and ascertain if they had any intentions towards him or if this was just a random encounter between strangers on the road. As soon as he entered the wood and was out of sight from those two men coming up behind him, Clancy spurred on the mare and left the track. Once he was among the trees, he reined in and, concealing himself a little behind a stout oak, waited to see what would chance next.

The two riders had evidently speeded up a little, because no sooner had Clancy moved off the track, than they rode into the afforested area. Once there, seeing that the man they had been pursuing was nowhere in sight, the two men reined in and looked about themselves, perplexed. Brent Clancy smiled to himself. It was just exactly as he had suspected; those boys were on his trail, although for why was a mystery to him. Then, to his surprise, one of the men called out amiably, 'Clancy! Where are you hiding, you son of a bitch?'

There was no menace in the question; both of the men had open and good-natured expressions on their faces and as he stared at them, it dawned on Clancy that he knew these two scamps. They were brothers and he had come across them from time to time. The older was called Jake, but he could not offhand recollect the name of the other. However, that did not signify because a moment later the man who had hollered out his name followed it up by shouting, 'Surely you remember us? Jake and Seb?'

Seb! That was it. He wondered that he could have forgotten the fellow's name, for the three of them had once worked together in a crooked poker game and rooked a couple of businessmen of a considerable sum of money. The only question that now needed to be answered was what those two boys were about and why they had been following him. He removed the pistol from where it was tucked negligently in his belt, cocked it with his thumb and rode forward. The cheerful greetings that they began to speak died on their lips when Jake and Seb Booker saw that Clancy was drawing down on them and looked ready to start a deadly contest, should need arise.

'Jesus, man,' cried Jake, 'What are you about? Thought we was old friends.'

'Why are you following me? What are you after?'

'That's soon told,' said Seb, 'Only put up your

weapon. It makes me nervous to talk under such conditions.'

It was true that in as far as people in their line of business could be friends, Jake and Seb Booker fell into that category and Clancy had no real cause to suspect the brothers of wishing to harm him. He lowered the hammer carefully and returned the Navy Colt to its usual position about his person. He said, 'Well then, what's the game?'

Both the brothers chuckled in the most good-natured and boyish fashion imaginable. Jake said, 'We were hoping to take down that stage. Got there just a mite too late. Watched you from the hill. Thought you'd blown your head off when that scattergun fired!'

'I hope you ain't trying for to cut yourselves in on the spoils?' said Brent Clancy, 'I took that stage fair and square.'

'Lord a mercy, Clancy,' said Seb. 'You never used to be so mistrustful and that's a fact. What ails you?'

The other man's open demeanour and pained look made Clancy feel momentarily ashamed and he covered this by saying wryly, 'You boys know how it is. You get so you don't trust nobody, not even other thieves.'

This sally elicited a whoop of laughter from the brothers and the tension was immediately dissipated. The three of them dismounted, led their horses into the trees, so that they would all be out of sight of casual travellers or unfriendly, prying eyes, and they sat down to take counsel together. The most remarkable thing about the Booker brothers was that they always seemed to be in a good humour. From the look of them right now, Clancy guessed that they were going through a pretty lean time, but their eyes were still sparkling with mischief and they were as good company as he recollected they had been when their paths had in the past crossed with his.

'Well, what's to do, lads?' asked Clancy. 'If you're not hoping to steal my pickings from holding up of that stage, why were you so keen to catch me up now?'

'Truth is,' said Jake Booker, 'Me and Seb ain't having the best time of it lately. Damn near got ourselves hanged just last week, when a bunch o' vigilance men came after us.'

'Hoo boy,' chipped in Seb, 'Was that something? I made sure we was going to get our necks stretched. Didn't get a cent out of the business neither. Robbing a bank in some piss-ant, little berg and a citizen had to intervene.'

'Yeah,' added Jake, 'Like it was his money or something. Well anyways, he got shot and we hightailed it out o' there and next thing they raise a posse to come look for us.'

Clancy shook his head sympathetically. Much the same thing had befallen him in the past. He said, 'They still on your track?'

'No, I reckon we's free of the toils, as it says in scripture.'

Patiently, Brent Clancy said, 'Listen you fellows,

this is all very interesting and you got my sympathy, but you ain't yet condescended to tell me why you were in such an all-fired hurry to speak with me today.'

'Well,' said Jake, 'Me and Seb, we got a plan. Only thing is, we need another body to help it along. Could make us a mint. You want in?'

Maggie Hardcastle could scarcely believe her good fortune. The pleasant gentleman who had been so concerned about her having no money and nowhere to stay had taken it upon himself to book her a room in the better of Indian Falls' two hotels. He was so courteous and deferential to her that Maggie was quite overcome. She was a shrewd soul and could generally sense when a fellow was hoping to take advantage of her, but she had no such apprehension about Mr Delaney. He was all solicitude and good manners.

After seeing that she was comfortably established in the Metropole, the man who had introduced himself to Maggie as Nathaniel Delaney asked diffidently if she would care to join him for a bite to eat. She was ravenously hungry and had already been wondering where her next meal would be coming from.

'I'll give you time to freshen up,' said Delaney, 'Perhaps if I knocked on your door in a half hour.' He looked remorseful and said hurriedly, 'Unless that strikes you as being improper, Miss Hardcastle? I shouldn't, of course, dream of actually entering a lone lady's room.'

Enchanted at such delicacy, especially after the goings on in the hurdy house in which she had been employed, Maggie giggled and replied, 'Oh, Mr Delaney, I wouldn't suspect a gentleman like you of improper suggestions! Please do call for me. And I hope that your head isn't too sore from that blow you took?'

'I had worse than that in the past.'

About five and twenty minutes after this conversation, there was a discreet tap on the door of Maggie Hardcastle's room. She opened it and was instantly bowled over as Nathaniel Delaney crashed into the door with his shoulder, causing it to swing open and strike her on the forehead, dazing her. Before she had recovered her senses, the man was in the room, locking the door behind him. His face was transformed; she wondered how her instincts could have played her so false. This was anything but a gentle, kind-natured man in his middle years. His face was that of a killer. It took Maggie only a second to come to this conclusion, but before she was able to scream for help, Delaney was upon her. He clamped his hand over her mouth and from somewhere produced a cravat or scarf. This he used to gag her, forcing open her mouth and then tying the thing behind her head, so that her jaws were held painfully open. The terrified girl expected to be taken advantage of, but instead, Delaney took a length of thin, supple rope from his jacket pocket and bound her hands behind her back.

Maggie Hardcastle was making frightened mewing noises through the scarf, sounding a little like a trapped animal. Delaney soothed her, saying, 'Just answer my questions, child, and you'll not be hurt. Try and fox with me though, and I promise you it'll go hard with you. You understand me?'

The girl searched Delaney's eyes, desperately trying to find some clue that would enable her to figure out the play. More importantly, she wanted to work out if this man was going to free her if she did as asked. Maggie had heard tales of men who enjoyed inflicting pain on helpless young women, sometimes to the point that their victims died. Was the man who held her at his mercy such a one as that? And he had seemed such a gentleman until a minute or so earlier!

For a slightly built man, there was a good deal of strength in the man calling himself Nathaniel Delaney. He stooped to the carpeted floor and swept up Maggie with as little effort as if she had been a kitten. Having laid her on the bed, he fetched a chair from the dressing table and set it down nearby. Following which he sat down, took out a gunmetal cigar case and carefully selected a cheroot. Being of base metal, Brent Clancy had not been bothered about the cigar case.

After striking a Lucifer and playing the flame delicately over the tip of his smoke until it glowed red, Delaney inhaled deeply and then expelled the smoke in twin jets from his nostrils. He puffed once more on the cheroot, before taking it from his lips, leaning over to the helpless girl and touching the red-hot tip against her hand. She squealed in pain and terror, but the gag made it unlikely that anybody else in the hotel, even in the corridor without, would have been able to hear a thing.

'I'm going to loosen the scarf, so that you can speak, but before God, if you cry out or scream for help, I'll burn up your face so bad that your own mother won't recognize you. Do we understand each other?'

The girl nodded eagerly. The last thing she had in mind was making this man angry. She wanted only to be freed. There were, she had discovered, worse things in this world than being penniless and alone in a strange town. Seemingly persuaded of her intention to cooperate, the man leaned forward and fiddled with the knot at back of her head. The relief of having her jaws freed from the pressure was exquisite. He gave her a minute to recover and then said quietly, 'I know that you are acquainted with that young fellow who knocked over the stage today. What's his name?'

'Clancy.'

'Given name or last name?'

'Last. His Christian name's Brent.'

'Good. This shouldn't take much longer. How do you come to know him?'

Maggie gave a brief account of the circumstances under which she had made Clancy's acquaintance. The man sitting before her listened carefully and then asked, 'Mark well, this is the most urgent consideration of all. Where was that boy headed?'

'He said something about the Indian Nations. He wasn't sure whether he was going to Kansas City or minded to head through the territories. Will you set me free now?'

'All in good time, my precious. Did this fellow mention any special route he would take. Think carefully now.'

The relief at the prospect of being released made Maggie Hardcastle feel a little faint. She said, 'All I can recollect is that he mentioned somebody called Abbot.'

'Joe Abbot would that be?'

'He didn't say. Just said he might drop by Abbot's place. Can I go now?'

Delaney said reassuringly, 'Yes, of course you can. But I'm going to have to put this scarf back before I leave. You see how I'm fixed, if you started hollering as soon as I leave, there might be unpleasantness. Don't fret though, I'll send somebody up from the lobby on a pretext and they'll free you. By then, I'll be long gone.'

So it was that Maggie didn't struggle or resist when the man about whom she had been so cruelly mistaken forced the scarf back into her mouth and tied it up again, although not so tight as before. She had been so scared, but now that the ordeal was over, a little extra discomfort like this meant nothing.

Once the scarf was securely in place, the man Maggie knew as Nathaniel Delaney wasted no more time. He lunged forward and placed both his powerful hands around the girl's throat, squeezing with all his strength. At first, Maggie's face went purple and suffused with blood and she wriggled back and forth, trying to alleviate the pressure, but it was all to no avail. It took a little under five minutes to kill the girl and by the end of the exercise, his hands were aching with cramp.

Frank Mason stood up and stretched his arms above his head in an effort to ease the pain from gripping the wretched young woman's neck for so long. Then he walked over to the window and gazed down to the street below. On the whole, he was moderately satisfied with what he had accomplished. He'd a good idea where that whelp was heading with his belongings and there was at least a strong chance anyway that the contents of the vanity case had not interested the robber. Mind, no chances could be taken with the Great Enterprise reaching its climax in just a few days.

Turning back to the bed, he observed with disgust that in her death throes, that cheap wench's bladder must have emptied, for there was a large and dark stain all across the counterpane. He lit another cheroot and then left the room.

Explaining the scheme that he and his brother had dreamed up, Jake Booker sounded to Clancy like some snake oil salesman. As Jake set out the case, the new railroad running through the Indian Nations would be an easy target for robbery. They could halt it at night by the simple expedient of swinging a red lamp as a signal of danger and then loot the passengers at will. Having heard the idea, Brent Clancy reserved judgement, saying merely, 'Well, I'll think on it. I'm guessing that you fellows are heading now into the territories, so our paths are like to run side by side for a while, whatever we decide.'

'You got plans of your own, Clancy?' asked Seb, 'Or you just drifting, same like usual?'

'Truth to tell, I'm getting kind o' tired of this way of life,' said Clancy slowly. He hadn't spoken to anybody about his feelings on this matter before; he was not in general much of a one for sharing his innermost thoughts with others. He continued, 'I was already after moving south, so we can keep company for a spell. If you're going for to hit that railroad, I suppose that you'll be stopping off at Abbot's place for vittles?'

'That was the idea, yeah.'

'How would it be then if the three of us rode south into the Indian Nations and then went as far as Abbot's and saw then how the scheme represented itself to us? I could do with company and three travelling together would make a group such as a lone operator might think twice about molesting or robbing. What do you boys say?'

It was plain from the look on their faces that the Booker brothers had hoped for something a little more definite than this and that what they really wanted was a firm commitment on Clancy's part to throw in his lot with them and embark upon what seemed to him, on the face of it, a mad and hazardous endeavour. He had no intention though of making a snap decision on something of that nature. Not only did many railroad trains have armed guards, Pinkerton men and so forth, there was always a risk from passengers who were heeled. No, such a venture would need the most careful consideration.

Seeking to soften his reluctance to agree at once to join in with the Booker brothers' plans, Clancy said cheerfully, 'Well boys, at the very least we'll get to ride together for a spell and catch up on old times. That's got to be worth something, hey?'

The native optimism of the Bookers returned to the fore and they smilingly agreed that catching up with an old friend was something to be valued, no matter how events panned out in the future.

CHAPTER 3

When, on 22 December 1865, Nathan Bedford
Forrest, one-time general in the army of the
Confederacy, had set out the bare bones of the
scheme that would lead to the restoration of
Southern Rights, he had left out certain vital details.
Those living in the defeated South had had ample
evidence of where a previous assassination of a president had led – to the oppressive military regime
under which they all currently suffered. Things had
been far worse for them after Lincoln's untimely
death than they had been before. What was to hinder
another set of assassinations from ending in an even
harsher military government of the southern states?
Seven of the nine men seated around the table in the
room above that saloon in Tennessee had pressed
General Forrest most forcibly and vociferously on
this very point, but he had refused to be drawn. He
simply asked if they trusted him as implicitly now as
they had done during the late war; which of course,
they did.

The only one whose voice had not been heard questioning the general that night had been Frank Mason. This was because, unknown to the others, Mason was the architect of the Great Enterprise and it would triumph or fail upon what he had been able to achieve. Mason knew also something of which none of the others, apart from General Forrest, had the least inkling. This was that there was a traitor at the very heart of the federal government in Washington and that the whole, entire scheme upon which they were staking their hopes, and perhaps even their very lives, would depend upon the successful treachery of this individual.

When the stage on which he had been travelling had been intercepted by a robber earlier that day, Frank Mason had been on his way to Indian Falls to meet up with a band of men who were part of the plan to restore the Confederacy to its rightful place among the nations of the world. The plan had been that they would immediately head north to Illinois, where President Johnson was due to make an unprecedented appeal to ordinary people as he battled to avoid impeachment. Everything was ready for the execution of one of the most audacious schemes ever seen, which would see the supposedly defeated southern states seize back control of their destiny from the Yankee oppressors. And now all these weighty matters had been cast into hazard by some young scoundrel who had made off with the only set of papers in existence that might, if correctly interpreted, enable a shrewd man to fathom out the whole enterprise! Well, there was only one remedy and that was to head south into the Indian Nations, find the boy, kill him and recover the documents.

Of course, it was a thousand to one against anybody being able to make any sort of sense of the various sketches, maps and plans that Mason had been carrying in his vanity case, but when a nation's destiny was at stake and with the finishing line so close, it would be absurd to take any chances. After strangling Maggie Hardcastle and smoking a final cheroot, Frank Mason went off to find his comrades and apprise them of the unfortunate circumstances that had arisen. He'd little doubt that before twenty-four hours had passed, they would have dealt efficiently with this trifling setback.

It was coming on towards late afternoon by the time that Brent Clancy and the Booker brothers had come to a tentative agreement on their next course of action; that is to say making their way together to Abbot's place in the territories. All else apart, they needed to put a little distance between the scene of the stagecoach robbery and their own selves, just on the remote off-chance that somebody in Indian Falls might take it into his head to put together a posse and ride out after the culprit. So it was that the three men set off after their meeting at a smart pace, heading south towards the Indian Nations.

After they had cantered along for a while, the three riders slowed down to a trot for a spell, which enabled them to have some more conversation. Jake

Booker said, 'Hand on heart Clancy, what do you think to this notion of ours, as touching upon taking down the Flyer?'

Brent Clancy considered for a few seconds before answering and then said slowly, 'If we could pull it off, I think it worth trying. Truly though, I'm affeared that there might be somebody riding shotgun, a body from Pinkertons or something of that nature. You follow me?'

'We ain't complete fools,' said Seb, with some asperity, 'We give that some thought, of course.'

'Where did all this thinking lead you?' asked Clancy ironically, 'For if I'm to be your partner in this, we need to share our ideas.'

But Seb Booker was offended and would say nothing more, other than, 'You want in Clancy, then we'll talk further on it. So far, you've blown hot and cold, and me and Jake'll keep our counsel 'til you tell us you're in for sure.'

Not wanting to fall out with the brothers and because he thought that there might be some merit in the projected robbery, Clancy smoothed things over, saying, 'Ah, Don't take on so! Let's see what the morrow brings and how we feel after we've reached Abbot's and got a hot meal in us. Happen we'll all feel a little more cheerful at that time and apt to talk.'

When it was too dark to ride safely any further, the three men camped in the lee of a craggy bluff, which jutted out from the surrounding plain. They had alternated cantering and trotting to some effect, covering something over fifteen miles by the time that night fell.

Clinging tenaciously to a rock face of the bluff was an ancient bristlecone pine and this the three of them managed to pull down and break up, so providing the makings of a modest campfire. Once the tinder-dry wood was blazing away merrily and providing a reasonable source of illumination, Clancy's curiosity finally got the better of him and he decided to see what the morocco-bound vanity case, for which a man had been prepared to risk his life, actually held. He felt slightly reluctant to go through the other proceeds of the robbery in front of Frank and Seb, for it might make them feel that they had been cheated in some way by somebody else taking down the stage that featured in their own plans. Clancy's desire to know what the case could contain that was worth dying for was, however, strong enough to overcome this slight scruple.

'What you got there?' asked Jake Booker, when once Clancy had gone over to his saddle-bag and fished out the vanity case. 'That looks a mite smarter than anything I'd expect you to be toting around, Clancy. I'll warrant you got it from somebody on that stage.'

'You got that right. It's what caused my face to get ploughed up by buckshot and I want to know what caused that fellow to act so.'

To Brent Clancy's surprise, the case held nothing of any value at all. The owner had been perfectly correct when he had said that it contained only papers, which were of no interest to anybody but him. There were sketches of a building, showing it complete and then in ruins. These were accompanied by measurements and notes about an explosion that had seemingly reduced it to the state shown in the second of the drawings. There were also a dozen pages covered in strange little squiggles, which Clancy took to be either some foreign language or perhaps a cipher. Then too, there was what looked like a map of a street. This was covered in strange, radiating lines from one side to the other. There was no indication where this place might be, other than a few of the squares, clearly meant to represent buildings, bearing cryptic notations. One, for example, bore a six-pointed star. Another, looking as though it were on the other side of the road from this, was labelled simply with a number seven; below which was a lozenge shape. Clancy could make nothing of this.

The two Booker brothers, evidently feeling some proprietary interest in the business, since they themselves so nearly had become the new owners of the vanity case, peered over Clancy's shoulder and made various observations. Clancy said, 'I wonder if this here, with the star, might signify one of those Jewish churches. You know, a what do they call 'em? Synagogues is it?'

Jake Booker laughed at that and replied, 'Synagogue, nothing! I know what that is. Know where it is, what's more.'

Seb peered harder in the flickering and uncertain light, before exclaiming, 'Hey, that's right. I know where that is for a bet.'

'The hell you do!' said Clancy, 'Care to enlighten me?'

'Don't see why not,' said Jake, 'That there star, it tells that it's the sheriff's office. Surprised at you Clancy, for not figuring that one out! And the seven, that with a diamond 'neath it, that's a saloon called the Seven of Diamonds. It's just across the way from the sheriff. Place is a gaming house really, which accounts for 'em naming it after a playing card.'

'Alright then,' said Clancy patiently, 'Where d'ye say this is?'

'Why, it's a little town up in Illinois, name of Terra Nova.'

Upon hearing this surprising piece of information, Brent Clancy felt as though he had received a sharp blow in his solar plexus. He said, 'You sure 'bout that, Seb?'

'Sure I'm sure. Ain't I right, Jake?'

'That you are. What's the matter with you Clancy? Look like you seed a ghost.'

Recovering his wits and realizing that it would not do to let that pair of scamps guess the real reason for his momentary discomposure, Clancy prevaricated skilfully, saying, 'It's just that I came across the name of that place only two days ago, is all. Seems like a rare coincidence.' He reached into his jacket and fished out a crumpled piece of paper, torn from a newspaper he had found lying around in the hurdy house in Sheridan. He handed this to Frank Booker and said, 'There! I call that odd, if you don't.'

46

The newspaper cutting was, according to the masthead at the top, from the *Sheridan and Chapman's Crossing Agricultural Gazette and Intelligencer* and it read as follows:

Those readers who favour the Democrat Party and support our current president, Mr ANDREW JOHNSON, will be pleased to learn that following his well-publicised difficulties with both the Republicans and members of his own administration, such as Secretary of War Mr EDWIN STANTON, President JOHNSON is taking to the hustings for the Congressional elections this year. If I said that following his accusing various respectable politicians of rank treason, the president hopes to 'drum up support'. It will be recalled that less than six months ago, in February, President JOHNSON gave a speech at the Whitehouse in which he rallied his supporters and astonished everybody by the claim that Pennsylvania Congressman THADDEUS STEVENS and Massachusetts Senator CHARLES SUMNER were so vehemently opposed to his policies that they were planning to assassinate him. These differences, combined with his fierce antipathy to members of his own government such as Mr EDWIN STANTON, have impelled the president to begin a nationwide tour, in which he will explain his aims to the population at large. This will begin on the 29th Inst. At the Illinois town of Terra Nova, where President JOHNSON believes that he might expect a fair hearing.

After the Bookers had read the piece from the news-paper, they allowed that it was somewhat of a coincidence. Thankfully, neither of them asked Clancy what his own particular interest in the town was, nor why he had troubled to tear out the cutting and keep it. After they had perused it, Clancy placed the paper back in his saddle-bag, where he kept a number of similar items.

There being nothing much for them to stay awake for, the three of them, by common consent, turned in early and agreed that if they rode hard, they should be able to cross into the territories the next day and perhaps even reach Abbot's place before dusk.

The greeting that Frank Mason received when he entered the saloon where he had agreed to meet his fellow conspirators was by no means a cordial one.

'Where the Deuce have you been, Mason?' said one of the roughest and most forthright of the men, 'We expected you two hours since.'

'I was unavoidably detained,' he replied smoothly, 'It couldn't be helped. Gentlemen, we have a problem.'

The noise in the bar-room was such that there was not the slightest apprehension of their being over-heard as the five of them talked in low voices in a partitioned space around a table. As Mason outlined the precise nature of the problem, the faces of the other four men grew grave. It was obvious that, like him, they were greatly concerned about the loss of the notes relating to the 'Great Enterprise'. Mason's behaviour could not be criticised, this was just a stroke of ill fortune. He said, 'We must all of us be in Terra Nova, two days from now, which is cutting things damned fine. But if those papers fall into the wrong hands, it could spell ruin for our plans, to say nothing of setting our necks at hazard. I say that we should all ride at dawn for the Indian Nations, find this boy and kill him. There's a new line running through the territories, it links up with the Union Pacific. We have time to ride south, take care of this matter and still be in Illinois in time.'

'I don't see that we have another choice,' said a swarthy-looking fellow with a faint French accent, 'We cannot risk betrayal.'

The others nodded their heads soberly and all of them agreed that they should get early to bed and start at first light for the territories. It was undeniably a nuisance, but with matters about to reach a climax, leaving those documents floating around in the hands of the Lord knew who was really not to be thought of.

Suspicions regarding the strange conduct of Secretary of War Edwin Stanton had begun swirling around almost before President Lincoln's body was cold. That the intention that April evening had been to kill all the major figures in the United States government was beyond doubt. Secretary of State Seward was stabbed in the throat as he lay in bed, at the same time that Lincoln himself was being shot in the theatre to which he and his wife had gone that evening. Other assassins had been despatched to kill Vice President Andrew Johnson at the same time. Stanton later claimed to have driven off a man who was trying to harm him as well, but nobody else saw this mysterious assailant. The actions of the secretary of war in the immediate aftermath of the president's death were certainly open to misinterpretation.

Without attempting to contact the vice president and find out whether or not he was alive, Edwin Stanton virtually declared martial law in Washington, sending troops to guard key points in the city. More than one observer remarked that the Secretary of War's actions that night looked to him very much like a military coup. Had Andrew Johnson actually been killed, which was the plan although he managed to evade death, then Edwin Stanton would undoubtedly have been in control of the nation for an indefinite period. As it was, Johnson, whom Stanton loathed, was sworn in as president and took the reins of power out of the hands of Secretary Stanton. The two men were bitter enemies ever afterwards.

It was partly to counter the intrigues and plotting of his Secretary of War, whom Johnson had been unable to remove, that President Johnson had announced his grand speaking tour. He may have had enemies in Washington, but he was convinced that he was beloved of ordinary people and wanted to give them a chance to see and hear him.

*

Brent Clancy lay on his back in the darkness, quite unable to sleep. He could hear the gentle snoring of the Booker brothers, who had seemingly fallen into the arms of Morpheus as soon as they had laid down and wished him goodnight. For his own part, Clancy had never been more awake or less able to close his eyes and drift off. Terra Nova! It had to be Terra Nova. For the last nine months or so, he had been seeing odd mentions of the town and had eagerly devoured any scrap of information that had come his way about it. He knew that very soon now, the councilmen of the town hoped to apply for a charter and have their town declared a city. He had read of the new manufactories there, which were making the town a byword of modernity. Most of all though, he saw mention of the renowned sheriff of Terra Nova; a man who was well known for his exploits before the war. In those days, he had been a US Marshal, of course, tracking down desperate criminals and either killing them or bringing them in to face justice. It was only natural that an up and coming town like Terra Nova should have wanted such a man to become its sheriff when peace returned.

One cutting that he kept in his saddle-bag mentioned the likelihood of the sheriff of Terra Nova turning to politics at some stage, when once he had hung up his gun-belt and handed in his star. He was after all still a relatively young man, despite all that he had so far managed to pack into his life. If he were spared, then Sheriff Grant Clancy would be just thirty-eight years of age this fall.

51

All his life, Brent Clancy had lived in the shadow of his older brother. His brother had been a deputy at the time that Brent was born. Nobody had been more surprised than their mother when, at the age of forty, she had fallen pregnant. Her family was complete and all but one of the children left home. Now, just when she thought that she could ease up a little, she was faced once more with the daunting round of diapers and child-rearing. Still, there it was. Prudence Clancy was not one to shirk her duties and she set to the task with grim determination, and if ever she felt some slight resentment towards the child who had come along so unexpectedly, then she hoped not to show it. Brent Clancy knew two things almost before he could walk and talk. One was that he had not really been wanted by his mother and the other was that he would need to work pretty damned hard to approach even remotely close to the standards set by his mother's first-born son, the famous Grant Clancy.

Throughout his childhood, Clancy had had the example of his big brother constantly held up before him. Even when Grant was prowling the country, running down malefactors, he always found time to recollect his filial duty and write letters home to his mother and father. These missives were read out loud by Mrs Clancy to her husband and younger son, and it was generally understood that the sentiments contained in them were invariably pious, elevated and correct. For in addition to being a lawman, his big brother was a lay preacher for the Methodist church and never let slip an opportunity of mentioning the will of the Deity and how it behoved us all to fulfil our duty towards Him. A natural and wholly unsurprising consequence of all these circumstances was that Brent Clancy reached adolescence with no favourable view of either lawmen or God. It came as a shock to nobody when he signed up as a soldier and immediately took to drinking, gambling, cursing and low company. It was no more than his mother had expected all along.

While Brent Clancy slogged away from battle to battle as a lowly infantryman, his brother gave up law-keeping for the duration and received a commission. The life of an officer was very different from that of a youngster in Brent's position and their paths did not once cross throughout the whole course of the war. While Grant continued to keep his mother apprised of all the wonderful things that he was doing and how he never passed up the chance to witness for the Lord, even on the very battlefield, Brent somehow felt little inclination to write long letters home. He limited himself to the occasional brief note, which was just sufficient to reassure his mother that he was still in the land of the living.

The war ground to its inevitable and tragic end and Grant left the Union army with fresh honours and plaudits, to become the sheriff of a town on the verge of becoming a city. His young brother turned to banditry and nobody, either in his own family or the world at large, was the least bit taken aback to see the very different roads that the two men took. It was understood by his mother's relatives and friends that she was immeasurably shocked by having a son on the scout, but that this was more than recompensed by having another boy who was renowned for being hot for both the Lord and the law of the land.

It was a strange thing, but for reasons that he could not really understand Brent Clancy had fallen into his mother's habit of clipping any mention of his brother's activities, or even the town where he was sheriff, from newspapers and keeping them with him. He was quite unable to say why he did that, but it accounted for his knowing about President Johnson's forthcoming visit to the town and also explained why he had been more than a little disturbed to find that the man he had robbed had some mysterious connection with the town of Terra Nova.

The next day dawned fine and mild. Clancy had fallen asleep in the end, but only fitfully and his repose was broken by a variety of vivid and unpleasant dreams. He was as a result not in the most amiable frame of mind that morning. There was little enough for the three men to break their fast on; a little dried jerky and the heel of a week-old loaf of bread. They were apt to be on short commons until they reached Abbot's place. The chances of coming across any provisions store in the wilderness that lay between them and their destination were vanishingly slender.

It was as they finished eating and were preparing to move out that Clancy had a sudden thought, followed swiftly by another, one of which was alarming in the extreme. His first thought was that it might be worth examining the pocket watch of the fellow to whom the vanity case had belonged. It might chance that there was an inscription or some such, something that would shed light on the man's identity. The second thought was the realization that he knew perfectly what was represented by all those lines drawn across the map of the street in which his brother's office was apparently situated, if the Booker brothers were to be believed, that is. It was a wonder he hadn't thought before, but these lines and cones were obviously meant to indicate lines of sight and, as a natural corollary, lines of fire, too. Combined with the notes and sketches relating to some explosion, it seemed to Clancy that some villainy might be planned for the town where his brother was charged with keeping order.

The watch seemed nothing out of the ordinary, the kind of Hunter that any well-to-do man might sport. It and the chain were made of heavy, old gold; Clancy guessed that it was scarcely alloyed at all. This would fetch a pretty price, if he was any judge of such things. Springing open the back showed nothing in the way of engraving, but after he had closed up the watch, Clancy noticed something that had evaded his attention until now. Attached to the 'T' at the end of the watch-chain was a tiny gold locket. It was barely half an inch across and at first he thought that it might be something to do with the Freemasons, who he knew identified each other sometimes by strange little trinkets and charms of this kind. As he began fiddling with it, Jake Booker came over and said,

'Thought you was in a rare hurry to move out at first light? What are you fooling around with there?'

'I don't rightly know. Something on the watch-chain of him as had those papers in his possession.'

'That's a right nice watch, Clancy. Looks to me like you done alright from that little bit of business you conducted yesterday.'

'Yes, and damned near had my eye shot out in the process. It wasn't a walk in the park, you know.'

By inserting his fingernail in the edge of the tiny piece of jewellery, Clancy succeeded in prising it open, to reveal nothing more than a white, enamelled disc, which bore some indecipherable black marks. He held the thing up close to his eyes and discovered that the marks were ornate calligraphy, which must have been executed by somebody equipped with a jeweller's glass. It took a moment or two for him to realize that he was looking at three letter Ks, linked intricately together.

'Well,' said Jake impatiently, 'What is it?'

Seb had come over to join them, wondering what the cause of the delay might be. His eyes were keener than Clancy's because he merely leaned forward and then grunted in recognition. He said, 'The Klan, by God. You surely know how to mix in the wrong company, Clancy.'

'Either of you know any other meaning behind a bunch of Ks set together like this,' asked Clancy, 'I'd say it was the Ku Klux too, but I don't want to be hasty.'

'Hasty, nothing,' said Jake Booker, who had also

been peering at the tiny disc and could now read for himself what was on it. 'I'd say nobody but a member of the Klan would have such a thing on his watch. Must be a devoted man too, you know. Membership is a hanging matter in the south.'

Clancy's face was grim and he said, 'I don't know but what I shouldn't do something about this. There's mischief afoot, I can feel it in my water.'

At these words, both the Booker brothers burst into quite genuine and unfeigned peels of merriment. Clancy shot them an angry glance and said, 'What's so all-fired funny, if you wouldn't mind telling me?'

'You are, you damned fool!' said Jake Booker, when he had caught his breath, 'You rob a man at gunpoint and now you're worried about his soul or what he might be doing with his life. What's it to you if he's in the Klan or not? You got his watch, ain't you? Lord, but you're a strange one sometimes, you know that?'

Short of owning that his brother was a lawman, which might have dented his reputation and made his fellow crooks look askance at him, there was no explanation that Brent could give about his anxieties. He accordingly stuffed the watch inside his jacket, along with the vanity case and put off thinking too deeply about it. Then he saddled up and rode south with the brothers, notwithstanding the fact that he was not easy in his mind and felt more than half inclined to turn back and make his way to Terra Nova to warn Grant that some trouble might be headed his way. But there, like as not his brother would send him packing and want nothing to do with Brent for besmirching the previous family claim! He would have to see how he felt about things in a day or two.

CHAPTER 4

Technically, no white men were allowed to settle in the territories of the so-called five civilised tribes, namely the Cherokee, Chickasaw, Choctaw, Creek and Seminole. This vast area, which later became the state of Oklahoma, was known variously as the territories or Indian Nations. In the years following the War Between the States, it was, of course, appropriated by the federal government and opened up to settlers. This was on the grounds that the five tribes had collaborated with the Confederates and their loyalty to Washington was therefore in doubt. Even before this though, there were a few white men living and working in the territories. One such was Joe Abbot.

In the spring of 1858, Joseph Abbot from Nebraska arrived in the Indian Nations with his wife, a Kiowa squaw. Nobody knew how and why Abbot had picked up with a woman of the Kiowa and since she spoke hardly any English and Abbot himself wasn't disposed to talk of the matter, this aspect of his life remained a mystery. He and his wife rode on a cart drawn by two oxen and piled high with their household goods. They halted for good in the heart of the territories and slept beneath the wagon until the pair of them built a wooden shack to dwell in. The location of this little hut was not chosen randomly. It was on a rocky slope, with a spring of fresh water near at hand. The perfect place, as Abbot saw it, for a trading post.

By some miracle, the Cherokee who lived thereabouts did not kill Abbot and his wife, and over the summer he set out the foundations for a modest house, which was to be built of the stones that were lying about the area in great abundance. These, he used to construct dry stone walls, caulked at first with mud, moss and twigs. It took the better part of eighteen months to construct, but in the end, he and his squaw had a modest house of such a size and construction as any farmer would feel satisfied to live in. Once they had moved into this handsome new abode, Joe Abbot dismantled their old shack and used the pieces to put together a kind of lean-to at the side of the building. This was to serve as a something along the lines of a Mexican cantina; a place where he would serve food and drink to white men who were travelling across the territories. While setting down roots in this way, Abbot and his wife scraped a living by selling cheap tin-ware, mirrors and trinkets to the Indians who came to trade. Every so often, he would take his cart off to a little town in Arkansas, where he would stock up on more goods to trade.

By 1866, what was known to one and all as 'Abbot's place' had become something of an institution for those passing through the territories. For white men, it was somewhere to get a hot meal and a shot of hard liquor, a place to catch up on gossip and news, a clearing house for information and a safe shelter for those riding on the edge of the law. Abbot never asked any questions, his one inflexible rule being that there was to be no gun-play in and around his establishment. The local Indians tolerated his presence among them because Joe Abbot provided them with all manner of goods, including firearms and whiskey, which they would otherwise find great difficulty in obtaining.

It was then only natural that three men on the scout like Brent Clancy and the Booker brothers should gravitate towards Abbot's place as a matter of course, certain-sure to pick up any intelligence relating to their projected enterprise of taking down the Flyer as it passed through the Indian Nations. That Clancy had confided to Maggie Hardcastle his intention of stopping off there though, had been an error that now looked as though it might prove the death of him, for it had been quite sufficient to put enemies on his track.

The morning was bright, Jake and Seb Booker were cheerful company and he had a fair sum of money in his possession. Despite all this, Clancy's mind was not easy. Why it should matter at all to him that some villainy might be planned for the town of which his sainted brother had charge was not clear to him. But then it was no stranger than the fact that he eagerly devoured any newspaper across which he came for news of Terra Nova or its sheriff! Who can understand the workings of the human mind where it touches upon our families?

Jake Booker said, 'Clancy, I declare you ain't heard a single word I said for the past half-hour, you know that?'

'I'm sorry. I'm just dreaming.'

'Still thinking about the Klan?'

'Maybe.'

The three men were riding roughly due south and found after a while that they were drawing close to the new railroad line, which ran almost precisely from north to south through the territories. They approached the line at a shallow angle and found that the track they were following ran parallel to the gleaming steel rails, which were to their right. They were heading down a slope that grew progressively steeper, causing Clancy to speculate that any railroad locomotive heading north would need to build up a good head of steam to tackle such an incline. It was while musing on this that he heard a faint cry of surprise from Frank Booker, who was immediately to his left. As he turned to see what had occasioned this, Clancy heard two other sounds. One was the mournful sound of a locomotive whistle in the distance and the other was the unmistakeable crack of musketry.

When Clancy looked at Jake Booker, it was not difficult to see why the fellow had sounded so surprised. He had been shot through the chest and was now slipping sideways from his mount; a circumstance that surely would have surprised anybody. A ball droned through the air, passing between Clancy and the man who was evidently mortally wounded, and soon after came the sound of another shot. When Clancy looked to see where the firing might be coming from, he saw that there was a little hillock perhaps a quarter of a mile from them, crowned by a stand of fir trees. A white puff of smoke was visible from this spot and it seemed to him that he could see some shadowy figures among the trees.

There are times when you can stand and fight and then again there are situations when the only rational course is to flee for your life. Clancy knew that his sawn-off scattergun would be utterly useless at such a range and beyond that, he had only the old single-action army Colt. From Clancy's perspective, this was a time to fly and he hoped that Seb would view matters in the same light. But Seb Booker had watched as his beloved brother had slid apparently lifeless from his horse and he didn't look to Clancy like a man who was accessible to reason. Seb spurred on his horse, drew his pistol and began firing as he rode straight towards the little copse from where men were shooting at him and Clancy. Brent Clancy decided that he owed no particular debt of gratitude to Seb Booker, certainly he himself had no obligation to sacrifice his life in order to be revenged for Jake's death. He accordingly turned around and set off at a smart canter in the opposite direction from where the gunfire was emanating.

When he glanced back, Clancy saw to his dismay that Seb was nowhere to be seen and that five riders were now bearing down on him. The men were spread out, obviously intent on riding him down, and judging from the way that they had opened fire without any challenge, their intention was most likely to kill him without further ado. They were in a bleak, flat, grassy area, with no cover beyond the occasional clump of trees. The plain stretched to the horizon and it wasn't hard to see how this was going to end, unless some other factor came into play. It was then that Clancy heard again the whistle of the railroad train, much louder than before. He looked back and saw that it was only thirty yards or so behind him.

Just as he had suspicioned, the locomotive was making heavy weather of the slope up which it was climbing. It was only gaining slowly upon him, which gave him the germ of an idea. It was a desperate one, but with those five men hot on his tail and clearly aiming for to kill him, it was a time when desperate measures were needed!

The men pursuing him were now no more than forty or fifty yards behind and they were gaining steadily upon Clancy. Presumably their horses were rested and fresh, to say nothing of being better beasts anyway than this old nag of his, which he had acquired for a song in Sheridan following a mishap with his previous mount. The locomotive was coming up now on his left and was no more than twenty yards behind him, narrowing the gap all the time. For a fleeting moment, Clancy hoped that some of the passengers might look from their windows and realize that they were witnessing an attempted murder, but then again, why should they? The men chasing him would be unlikely to fire at him until the train had passed out of sight, and to anybody watching the pursuit might look like some kind of playful lark between a bunch of high-spirited men. Certainly nothing to operate the emergency brake for!

The train was now barely a dozen feet behind Clancy, coming up behind his left shoulder. It was now or never and he suddenly lurched to the left; hoping that his horse would not stumble as it crossed the rails. The creature didn't like having the thundering locomotive so close, but it did as it was bid and now Clancy had the length of the railroad train between him and his pursuers. He drew his feet from the stirrups and endeavoured at the same time to maintain the same speed. The horse did not care at all for the close proximity to the train and Clancy had to keep pulling the reins to the right to ensure that he remained close enough for his purposes. The slope up which they were travelling was beginning to level out, which caused the train to begin drawing ahead with ever greater speed. It was now or never.

While still keeping the horse as close as could be to the racing train, Brent Clancy drew up first one leg and then the other, until he was crouching on the saddle. Almost immediately, the beast began to slow down. He had been urging it on frantically before with his knees and spurs and once that encouragement abated, there was a slackening off of effort. The carriages containing people moved past at an alarmingly speedy pace and now the three freight vans were moving swiftly along on his right-hand side. There would only be one chance at this and if he failed then he would be dead in seconds. The horse was, despite Clancy's frantic tugging to the right, beginning to move away from the train and so he took a deep breath and simply leapt at the gap between the last of the freight vans and the guard's van at the rear.

He landed heavily on the coupling between the two coaches and for an instant, his leg trailed down towards the tracks and Clancy thought that the rest of his body was about to follow and he would end up being mangled beneath the wheels. It didn't happen though and, despite being greatly winded by the fall, he was able to secure himself by clinging hard to the metal coupling. Then he managed to sit up and, peering back, he was delighted to see that the five riders were unable any longer to keep up with the train's rapidly increasing pace, now that it was on the level ground again. They had reined in and even at the distance he was from them, he could sense the baffled fury that they felt at being cheated of their prey.

There was a hatchway leading into the freight van, through which, after prising open the wooden flap, Clancy succeeded in crawling. He found himself in a gloomy space piled with boxes, barrels and luggage. There was a small exit at the far end of the van, which enabled him to cross the coupling and reach the next van. In this way, he reached the passenger coaches and, after dusting himself down a little, he entered the main body of the train and contrived to look like an ordinary traveller who had paid for his ticket like everybody else. Finding a vacant seat, he sank into it with relief. The realization that he had come closer to death in the last hour than at any time since the end of the war gradually sank in and Brent Clancy knew that he had to think very carefully about his steps over the coming days.

By starting at four in the morning, when the first glimmer of false dawn was lightening the eastern sky, and riding hard, Frank Mason and his companions had managed to reach a spot roughly equidistant between the scene of the ambush on the coach heading to Indian Falls and Abbot's place. It had been a calculated gamble that at first seemed to pay off gloriously. Mason had seen the boy who robbed him, opened fire and, missing his target, taken down one of the others with whom the young robber was riding. Then the other man had ridden straight for Mason and the others and been shot down in his turn. All that remained was to chase down the man they actually hoped to kill, recover Mason's belongings from his corpse and then make their way to Terra Nova. If it hadn't been for that cursed train arriving, almost as though by appointment, they would surely have accomplished their end.

Now, the five of them had dismounted after catching the horse that had been abandoned and were busily engaged in going through the saddle-bag for any clues that were to be found. It was Mason who found the sheaf of flimsy paper, torn from various newspapers. The top one sent a chill through him. He showed it to the others, saying, 'There's more to this matter than first appears. See here!'

'You reckon he was on your track before he held up that stage?'

One of the others was leafing through the other cuttings and observed, 'It's not just about Johnson's visit. That fellow has some interest in the sheriff of the town. I don't like this one bit.'

Frank Mason said thoughtfully, 'I'll own as I'm a little taken aback here. But it don't alter in any degree our course. I'll warrant that for whatever reason, that young fellow'll be making now for Terra Nova.'

'Yes,' said one of the men, 'To alert that sheriff to our schemes, no doubt.'

'Maybe,' replied Mason, 'but see here what the sheriff's own name is? He's also a Clancy. Mark what I say, there's a family connection.'

'You think as he's guessed what's afoot and is now scuttling off to Terra Nova with the news?'

'Happen so, but there's no solid evidence in those papers. I don't see President Johnson cancelling his speech there. If needs be, we'll just take out the sheriff first. Should be easily done, when so much is at stake.'

'I should just about say that there's a lot at stake,' remarked one of the company who had not yet spoken. 'We all stand to have our necks stretched if this miscarries.'

'You think I forgot that?' asked Frank Mason, turning to glare angrily at the last speaker. 'I got as much to lose as any of you and I say that matters are not hopeless. We were headed for Terra Nova in any case, so that plan ain't altered. We aim to kill that boy too, so that's not changed either. All this means is that we might be well-advised to kill this sheriff, too. Which, considering what we're playing for, is no more than straw in the wind.'

'What now then?'

'There's a little way-halt north of here. There's twelve hours 'til the next train through the territories and I hope for us to catch it. With luck, they'll be able to take our mounts, too. In any event, we race to Terra Nova and then see how things stand. Long as we're there a day or two before Johnson. Once that fish is fried, we're home and dry.'

Because Secretary for War Edwin Stanton was such a taciturn and uncommunicative man, having few spoken words to spare even for his friends and none at all for his many enemies, it had not yet been noticed that his mind was disturbed and that he was suffering from a subtle and hard-to-detect kind of madness. This manifested itself not in the afflicted man raving or throwing off his clothes and dancing under the moon, but rather in his embarking upon a course of action that no rational and sane individual would for a moment contemplate. This was the only explanation possible for the fact that the very man charged with the guarding of the government and protection of the Union from enemies had taken it into his head to participate in a treasonable conspiracy whose aim was nothing less than the destruction of the United States of America.

A few days before the terrible War Between the States ground to its inevitable close, with the victory of the Union army, the man in overall charge of the federal forces, under the president of course, received word from a reliable source that an attempt was to be made on Mr Lincoln's life. The information was that not only the president was to be assassinated, but also Vice President Johnson and the Secretary of State. Although Lincoln had entrusted Stanton largely with the conduct of the war, the two men had never really cared over-much for each other. By 1865 Stanton had decided that his own ambitions lay in running the country, but he had now turned fifty and knew that he was not a popular figure. It would be impossible for him to command enough support to stand for president, at least with Lincoln blocking his path. However, if Lincoln, Johnson and Secretary of State Seward were all to be removed, then Stanton would be in a position to declare martial law and take over the running of the country, *de facto* if not strictly speaking *de jure.*

In the event, only Lincoln had died that fateful April night. Before he knew that the assassins had bungled their business, Stanton had called out the army and was in a fair way to assume power in Washington. He had it in mind to declare a state of emergency the following day and then to suspend the constitution, but of course that wretch Johnson had upset the apple cart by turning up unharmed and having himself proclaimed president, which was constitutionally quite correct.

Fifteen months later, Stanton sat brooding in his Washington home, as Brent Clancy, Frank Mason and President Johnson were all making their way to Illinois, and the Secretary of War felt that power was now within his grasp. He had had dealings, at arm's length as you might say, with some southerners who wished only for the end of military rule in the conquered states of the south. They had promised to remain in the Union and to live peaceably under the nominal rule of Washington. Stanton for his part wanted all the troops he could muster, for when he made his play for power.

Of course, neither side in this Devil's bargain trusted the other. For his part, Edwin Stanton was already thinking that once he was established as undisputed leader of the Union, backed by the army, then there would be nothing to hinder him from sending his army south again if the mood took him. For their part, the southerners who had given such solemn assurance of fidelity to the Union were in private considering how long they would have to leave it after the military withdrawal before they were able to secede once more from the Union. For the time being though, Stanton and the leaders of the Klan needed each other and it was in the interests of both parties that President Johnson died violently as speedily as could be neatly arranged.

'You're a rascal!' said the old woman sitting opposite Brent Clancy. He looked up in surprise, uncertain what reply to make. The woman chuckled and continued, 'You think I didn't see you fleeing those fellows? You buy a ticket for this here train before you boarded it?'

'You going to lay an information against me to the guard?'

'It's no affair of mine. See you sitting there though, like butter wouldn't melt in your mouth! What happened to your horse, you leave him behind?'

'I was in somewhat of a hurry. It couldn't be helped.'

The old woman laughed again and said, 'Somewhat of a hurry? I should just about say you were. I saw those fellows chasing after you! Where you headed, son?'

'Illinois. Town called Terra Nova. You hear of it?'

'Sure. You'll need to leave this train when we reach the junction in a few hours. Then get another train heading east. Take you right to Terra Nova. You in trouble?'

For some reason, Clancy thought that he could trust this woman and he said honestly, 'I reckon so, yes.'

'You're powerful young. You don't look like a regular villain neither. Got anybody waiting for you in Illinois?'

'My brother's the sheriff there.'

'You think he'll welcome you? He know you're coming?'

So shrewd was the old woman that Clancy suddenly smiled for the first time since holding up the stage. He said, 'My brother and me, we haven't had too much to do with each other in recent years.'

'Well,' said the woman, as the train began braking, preparatory to coming to a halt, 'I got to leave here. You just remember that family is all you got. All you can depend upon when the chips are down. Good luck to you, young man.' She stood up and then, to Clancy's surprise, leaned over and kissed him on the top of his head.

The encounter with the pleasant old woman was strangely cheering to Clancy and his good humour lasted all the way to Terra Nova. He changed trains where the woman had indicated he should and this time paid for a ticket right through to his destination. It was a mercy that Clancy was accustomed to keeping cash-money on his person, rather than in his saddle-bag, and he had enough from the robbery to tide him over for a little while yet. He had lost two of the watches he had lifted, which had been in the saddle-bag, but had with him the most important one; the one with the Klan insignia on it. He'd an idea that he would need all the evidence he could produce if he was going to persuade his brother that he was in earnest.

For all that he'd been reading about Terra Nova for the last year or more, the reality of the town took Clancy a little by surprise. He'd seen where the place was hoping to apply for a charter to become a city in the next year or so, which had led him to suppose that it was a large and bustling town. It certainly didn't strike him that way when the train pulled into the depot. All he saw when he stepped down from the train and left the depot was a typical little town of the kind with which he was perfectly familiar. The main street was perhaps a little smarter than most and the wooden buildings were giving way to those built of brick and stone, but otherwise there appeared to Clancy to be nothing especially note-worthy about Terra Nova.

What made Terra Nova so important and had set it on its path to cityhood was that the head of the coun-cilmen had instituted strict zoning regulations to control the growth of industry in and around the town. Those wishing to set up manufactories had received every encouragement and incentive to do so, bringing splendid opportunities for employment to those living in the surrounding countryside. New houses were being constantly thrown up for such newcomers to inhabit, but there were strict rules, which were rigorously enforced, to maintain pleas-ant, residential areas and keep them separate from the foundries and factories that belched out their noisome fumes three miles away on the very edge of the town's limits. Attracting industry to Terra Nova

had been a right smart move and, although he didn't
yet know it, Brent Clancy's brother Grant had been
instrumental in the policy that had made the town
such an up and coming place. It was little wonder
that President Johnson had chosen to make the first
speech of his campaign here, because this Illinois
town symbolised the future of the United States as an
industrial power.

As he strolled along Main Street, keeping a watch-
ful eye out for the sheriff's office, Clancy began to
notice one or two differences between this town and
others that he had visited since the war ended.
Everything here was a good deal cleaner and neater
than usual. Even the people looked smart and well
turned out; like they were on their way to church or
something. This was a place where the citizens made
a particular effort to keep up appearances. There
were no drunks about nor, as far as he could see, any
loafers or drifters. Most of the storefronts were shiny
clean and many looked as though they had just lately
been painted. Clancy caught a few odd looks from
those he passed and realized that with his dusty and
bloodstained clothes, to say nothing of the bloody
scab marking his cheek, he must present an unwel-
come contrast to most of the other passers-by.

The sheriff's office was only a half mile or so from
the depot and, when he reached it, Clancy glanced
down the street and, sure enough, saw that there was
a saloon called the Seven of Diamonds just across the
way. There was little purpose in delaying what was
likely to prove a trying and disagreeable encounter

and so he didn't pause, but just opened the door and walked right into the office.

Although he hadn't seen him in a good, long while, Brent Clancy recognized his brother immediately. He could have picked out that smug and self-satisfied visage under any circumstances. He greeted his brother cheerfully, saying, 'How's it going, brother?'

Grant Clancy didn't reply for a moment. He was too busy in running his eyes over his younger brother's appearance and, from the look on his face, forming an unfavourable impression of the same. This was confirmed when the sheriff, who was alone in the office and seated at a perfectly tidy and well-ordered desk, said, 'You surely look a disgrace. What brings you here?'

Brent was tempted to make a sharp response to this, but felt that it would hardly make matters better. Instead, he said slowly, 'I have evidence of what looks to me like some kind of plot. Involves this town and so I thought I ought to warn you of it.'

Sheriff Clancy did not unbend, but continued to stare disapprovingly at his brother. He said, 'This plot, as you call it, you looking for reward money or aught of that kind?'

'You going to invite me to sit down, so I can set out the case for you? I've an idea that we don't have a heap of time.'

'There's no "we". I don't know what you're about, but I tell you now if this is some scheme to make a profit at my expense . . . well it had better not be, that's all.'

After the trying time that he had had over the last few days, Brent Clancy had had enough of this. He walked over and sat down opposite his brother, saying as he did so, 'Same self-righteous son of a bitch as ever you were, I'm sorry to observe. Well, it can't be remedied, I guess.'

CHAPTER 5

There was a deadly silence in the office and the tension and hostility between the two brothers lent the atmosphere an electric feel, as one sometimes feels before a thunderstorm. Neither seemed inclined to speak for a few seconds, just staring one at the other. At last, Brent Clancy said wearily, 'This is nothing to the purpose. I'll show what I have and you make of it what you will.' He reached into his jacket and pulled out the morocco-bound vanity case, opened it and then handed the papers within to his brother, saying, 'This looks like a sketch map of this street.'

Grant Clancy went through the various papers thoroughly; scrutinising the map and then reading the description of the explosion and effects of the fortified nitro. After a few minutes, he said, 'Anything else?'

Without speaking, his brother took out the heavy, gold watch and opened the little charm on the chain. Having done this, he handed it to Grant, saying, 'By the look of it, this is tied in with the Klan.'

After examining the enamelled disc, the sheriff looked up and said, 'Where did you get this?'

'Took it off a man.' Replied his brother coolly.

'Stole, I suppose you mean.'

'I didn't have to come here, you know. Soon as I found this was about Terra Nova, I came straight here to warn you. Well, I done so and I reckon that's it.' He began to rise.

'You know our mother's dead?'

Although he'd not seen her in the better part of a year and they had not parted on cordial terms, the news still came as a shock. Grant Clancy said, 'She wanted to see you at the end, but we didn't know where you was to be found.'

'How long since?'

'Two months. A little more.'

'Did she suffer?'

'Pain, you mean?' asked Grant Clancy, 'Sure she did. It was a cancer, woman's thing. Ate her up 'til she was screaming in agony. Nothing the doctor did could help.'

They sat there without speaking, this time not in hostility, but a shared grief. Brent said, 'What about Pa?'

'You know how he depended upon here. He's a broken man. Sits there all day, doing nothing but grieving for her.'

'You think as I should go by the house to visit?'

Sheriff Clancy shrugged and for the briefest moment, it looked as though a smile might be about to flicker at the corner of his lips. He said, 'It's a good long while since you asked any advice of me, Brent.'

'What do you make of this here? There's more.' He gave a short account of being ambushed on the way to Abbot's place. 'I thought it might be connected with this business. I'd take oath I saw the man whose watch and papers these are among them as attacked me and killed my friends.'

Grant Clancy sighed and said, 'Like I don't have enough to occupy me, what with this visit from the president and all. Still, you're right. There's something here needs to be looked into. You got somewhere to stay in town?'

'Not hardly. I come here straight from the depot.'

'You can't walk around town looking like some kind of scarecrow. You're all over blood as well, you know that? What happened to your face?'

'It's nothing.'

'We're still about the same size, I guess. I reckon you can borrow some o' my clothes. But you listen to me good, Brent. I've worked hard to bring this town up to scratch. I aim to run it one day as mayor, God willing. Long as you're here, you'll behave like a normal person, you hear what I say?' Grant shook his head and said, 'I guess I'll have to own you as my brother to others. Try not to be a reproach to me, hey?'

Johnny West had been vastly impressed by the demolition of the old mission station. Just ten gallons of that oily sludge had wrought more destruction than

80

he would ever have dreamed possible. All that was now necessary was for Johnny to escort to Terra Nova the fellow who would mix up the nitroglycerine that they would need to take out the president and his entourage.

Nitroglycerine is really nothing more than a mixture of nitric and sulphuric acid, combined with a little glycerine. The ingredients can be obtained at any drugstore, but getting them to combine in the right proportions, without blowing up in your face, is the Devil's own job. You need ice to cool it down, a perfectly clean laboratory and the steadiest nerve in the world. Once you have your basic nitro, it is possible to add black powder to it, to boost the power of the explosion. This sort of preparation was sometimes marketed under the proprietary brand name of 'Black Hercules'.

A few months earlier, on 21 April to be precise, a large barrel of nitro had been shipped to the Wells Fargo office in San Francisco. It had begun leaking and then, because it is such an unstable and hazardous material, the whole lot went up in a devastating explosion that took out most the city block upon which the Wells Fargo office was situated. This disaster had prompted new laws to be rushed through in every state in the Union, forbidding the transportation of nitroglycerine on railroads and ships and also setting severe restrictions upon where it could be manufactured or used. This was particularly unfortunate for the men planning to assassinate President Johnson as it meant that they would either have to buy it from some shady customer who might then betray them, for a price, to the federal government, or to find somebody who could make it for them where it would be used. This man's life would be worth less than nothing when once he had accomplished his purpose and supplied the Klansmen with the ten gallons that they required.

Johnny West was not at all keen on the little man whom he had to bring to Terra Nova. For one thing, the fellow was a drunk, who had the shakes each morning until he had had a shot or two of whiskey. He had been previously employed by the Chesapeake and Ohio Railroad as an engineer in charge of preparing and using nitro to blast a pass though some mountainous terrain, but his drinking had got so bad that there was a general fear that it was only a matter of time before he bungled his work and blew the whole camp to kingdom come. He had been discharged and then recruited by Frank Mason to come and do a little private work for some southern gentlemen.

West and Jed Taylor, the one-time railroad engineer, were seated opposite each other in a passenger coach of a railroad train that was now only an hour or so from Terra Nova. Johnny West noticed to his disgust and alarm that although it was not yet evening Taylor was already three parts intoxicated. It was West's given job to supervise this hopeless drunk in manufacturing the nitro needed to destroy the civic hall that stood opposite the Seven of Diamonds. Just how he was going to achieve this end, Johnny

West had little idea. It would be a mercy if they were not all blown to atoms before President Johnson even showed his face in Terra Nova. For about the fiftieth time since they had boarded the train, Taylor began fidgeting and twitching, as though somebody had dropped a scorpion down his neck. He was, thought Johnny West, displaying all the signs of an inveterate inebriate deprived of access to intoxicating liquor. He stared coldly at the wriggling man and said in a low voice, 'What ails you, man? Stop jiggling about, you're making an exhibition o' yourself.'

'I can't help it,' muttered the wretched man, 'I always get this way, less'n I have a little something in the morning to get me started.'

'Lord a mercy, you best have a steady hand over the next few days, you hear what I tell you?' exclaimed Johnny West irritably. Then, recollecting that it would not do to draw any attention to themselves, he said in a lower voice, 'Soon as we get to Terra Nova, you can have a "little something" to steady your nerves, all right?' He looked at the pitiful wreck sitting opposite him and thought what a dreadful curse liquor could be to some. Jed Taylor could scarcely have been above forty years of age, but looked like a wizened and shrivelled up old man. Then he suddenly felt sorrow for anybody capable of doing such a dreadful thing to his own self and said to the shivering man, 'Don't take on so. We'll be in Terra Nova soon and you can get to a saloon or something. Long as you're ready to set to work tomorrow, mind.'

The killing of the sheriff of Terra Nova would need to be timed just right, thought Frank Mason, as he and the others waited for the Flyer. Some enterprising soul had set up a little canteen at the way halt where they were fixing to catch the train, which meant that at least they now had some coffee and vittles in their bellies.

The landscape hereabouts was windswept and bleak. As far as the eye could see, there was nothing but grass and a few spindly trees. How folk were able to live in such a Godforsaken spot was a mystery to Mason; he was city bred and liked to have plenty of stores, gambling houses and saloons around him. Open spaces made him uneasy. He reached for his watch and then stopped; recalling that he no longer had one. That too was a score to settle with that young thief. Murdering the boy who had stolen his watch might well be a matter of strict policy and necessary in order to protect from discovery the Great Enterprise, but it would also be a matter of personal satisfaction to Frank Mason.

Since only he and his companions were waiting for the arrival of the railroad train and they were standing some distance off from the canteen, Mason felt that they could discuss their projected actions without fear. He said, 'You're sure that young hotblood will be able to take care of Taylor and get him safe to town?'

One of the other men laughed and said, 'I'd trust

Johnny West with my life, but he surely has a hard row to hoe this time and no mistake! That Taylor is a sodden wretch, but he knows his stuff. If Johnny can keep him sober enough for a day or two, it'll all be fine.'

'But you think that West is the boy to make sure that the man gets there on time,' persisted Mason, 'For if he don't, I tell you now that the whole thing will miscarry.'

'You're a worrier, Mason,' said another of the men, 'Allus were. You're a damned good soldier, but you worry too much. If Johnny West said that he'd bring Jed Taylor to Terra Nova, then that's what he'll do.'

'I surely wish we could o' got somebody other than an inveterate barfly to act for us in this matter,' opined Mason gloomily, 'The timing is key to everything and drunks are apt to be late or not show at all. Leastways, that's been my own experience.'

'We had to take what we could get,' said one of the others, who had not yet spoken. 'We was lucky to find Taylor, after he was discharged by the 'C' and 'O' road. The old Chesapeake and Ohio line, you know? What was your idea on the subject, Mason? Advertise in the local newspaper, maybe? How about, "Smart fellow wanted to help destroy the Union; must be dab-hand with preparing explosives".'

'You're funny and I don't think,' growled Mason, 'I only hope we won't repent of using a soak like Taylor, that's all I say.'

Far away in the distance came an eerie wailing, like some discontented spirit bemoaning its fate. All five of the men became suddenly alert and began to prepare themselves for boarding the Flyer. Frank Mason said, 'So we agreed? We kill the boy as soon as we set eyes upon him and the sheriff just as soon as Johnson is readying himself for his speech?'

Since there had not really been any sort of agreement on this, the others looked across at Mason and gave non-committal grunts and shrugs. A terrible worm of anxiety was gnawing away at Mason. He was, as the other man had remarked, one of nature's worriers, but in the present instance, he truly felt that he had cause to fret. The wholly unlooked for circumstance of the robbery to which he had been subjected had not only put him out of countenance, but, he truly believed, had set all their plans at hazard. Only when Brent and Grant Clancy were both lying dead would he be able to breathe a little easier.

As they walked together down Main Street, presumably in the direction of his brother's home, Brent Clancy noticed again how neat and tidy everything looked. He remarked as much to Grant, who said, 'There's a town ordnance which requires all the stores to paint their fronts once a year. Not just with creosote either. If they want a prime site on this street, they have to paint their fronts properly. Same as the sidewalk outside their places, they're all legally responsible for it, has to be swept clean twice a day.'

'That your idea?'

Grant shrugged and said, 'Times are changing, you know. Now the war's over, folk want something different. They're after peace and prosperity. I aim to bring this town to order, make it a place where a man can raise his children and know that they'll be safe, that his wife can walk down the street without being bothered.'

In the usual way of things, this was precisely the attitude of his brother that Clancy had been accustomed to dismiss as prissy and schoolmarmish, but, walking along the pretty little street now, so different from many of the towns that he had been in, he was not so sure. There was a pleasant and welcoming feel about the place and it was nice to see brightly coloured storefronts rather than the dreary browns and greys that one saw elsewhere.

Then too, there were many old barrels that had been sawn in half and planted with crimson geraniums and sweet, white alyssum. Even passing by these, Brent could smell the sweetness of the alyssum. He said, 'Do you fine 'em if they don't plant flowers?'

Ignoring the faintly mocking tone, his brother replied, 'No, that was the idea of those as have stores along here. It brightens up the place considerable. Makes folk linger on the sidewalk and gaze into windows more than they might do else.'

Brent felt a little ashamed for sneering at something so agreeable and said reluctantly, 'Well, I'll own that this here street is a deal more attractive than many I've seen.'

They were passing a saloon and just as they

reached the bat-wing doors, a burly man came cannoning out as though he had been shot from a catapult. He landed in a heap in the dusty roadway and, as the two brothers stopped to watch, got unsteadily to his feet, dusted himself off and then, from inside his jacket, produced a small pistol. Then he began marching back towards the doors of the saloon, clearly intent upon wreaking violence upon somebody.

It was Brent Clancy's habit to step aside from all incidents of this kind, as being none of his affair. His brother though, being sheriff of the town, could not afford to adopt such an attitude. Without making a great thing of it, Grant strolled over to the doors of the saloon and obstructed them with his body. When the man brandishing the firearm approached, it was plain that he was as drunk as a fiddler's bitch and Brent wondered what would chance. He knew that his brother was a hard man, but was he really prepared to risk his life for such a trifling matter?

The drunk squared up pugnaciously and said, 'You best move out o' my way, Clancy, if'n you know what's good for you, that is!'

'I know you, Jem Carter, and you know me,' said Terra Nova's sheriff quietly, 'Why, I even attended your boy's christening, if you'll recollect. You want to end up in gaol or worse, leave that little one without a father to care for his family? That what you want?'

At mention of his baby son, the mood of this menacing fellow with a gun in his hand changed abruptly and he became lachrymose and maudlin, saying, 'My little boy, left alone. What would become of him and his ma?' He gave a sob.

'Well now, things ain't reached that stage yet,' said Grant Clancy, consolingly, 'I'm not about to run you in, for all that you know how much I dislike to see folk waving firearms around on the public highway.'

It was clear that the thought of his son being left without a protector had quite overcome the man who, a moment earlier, had been intent upon murder. He was at that stage of drunkenness when it would not take much for him to start bawling like a child.

'Tell you what, fellow,' said Grant, 'You just hand me that pistol, real peaceable like, and then go home to your family, I reckon as I can see my way clear to forgetting all about this piece of foolishness. You can have it back in the morning you know.'

'You ain't going to run me in?'

'Not a bit of it. Come now, let me have that weapon and you go home and have a nice sleep.'

'I'm sorry. Real sorry.'

And to Brent Clancy's unutterable amazement, that was the end of it. The hulking great brute of a man, in his cups and with violence in his heart, simply handed his gun to Grant, who patted him amiably on the shoulder and told him to call by the office the next day to collect it. It was one of the bravest and most extraordinary things that Brent Clancy had seen in a good long while. After they had moved off, he said to his brother, 'That was something else again, you know that?'

'What, getting Jem to go home and sleep it off? What do you say I should have done, arrested him and brought disgrace upon him and his family? He's a good fellow at heart and tomorrow he'll be as contrite as can be. He'll remember it, what's more. I don't want enemies, Brent. I want friends. Makes for a better sort of town for us all.'

'It's just knowing how down on drink you are, I'd o' thought you might have come down real heavy on him, that's all.'

Grant Clancy shrugged and replied, 'Just 'cause I don't want to get liquored up, doesn't mean that nobody else should. We're all different. Here, we're home.'

At the gate of the pretty little garden that surrounded the white-painted, clapboard house, the sheriff paused. He said, 'Listen, I guess I don't have to tell you that I don't look to hear cursing or see any unbecoming behaviour in front of my family? We understand each other well enough on that score?'

Feeling very much like the kid brother, Brent said stiffly, 'Yes, you need not tell me so. It's understood.'

By the summer of 1866, with the mid-term elections looming, President Andrew Johnson was feeling very much as though he was at bay; a hunted animal cornered by a pack of dogs. Which was, he reflected that evening, as he sat brooding in his library, a preposterous state of affairs for the leader of a great nation! Even though he was in charge of the whole country and did not even have a vice president to contend with, he was still unable to dislodge that worthless scoundrel Stanton from his post as Secretary of War! It was absurd.

Accusing Congressman Stevens and Senator Sumner earlier that year of planning to assassinate him had been an inspired move, summoning up, as it did, the remembrance of poor dead Lincoln. People said that his speech in February had been hysterical, but they would soon discover how wrong they were after he hit the campaign trail in Illinois. Choosing Terra Nova had been a right smart idea, for it symbolised all that he thought good about America since the war. With luck, the ordinary people of the country would see what sort of a man their president was, just one of them really, and they would rally around him and give him sufficient authority to get rid of that viper Stanton once and for all.

In two days' time, Johnson, along with Secretary of State Seward and various other important people, would leave Washington and head for Illinois. From there, he and his entourage would travel across the length and breadth of the United States, showing everybody that they had a strong and capable leader and that it was he, not Stanton and General Grant, who was running the country. As soon as the tour was over, he would return to the capital in triumph, sack Stanton, dismiss Grant and then he could get on with governing.

The railroad clerk looked dubiously at the crates that

Johnny West was unloading from the freight coach. He said, 'They're heavy enough. What you got in 'em son?'

'Pharmacy stuff. Special liquid.'

Mindful of the recent disaster in San Francisco, the old man said, 'You ain't trying for to bring any of that nitro into my depot, I suppose?'

This was so near the mark, that for a moment West was quite taken aback. He gulped and did not know what to reply. It was all right though, for the clerk suddenly chuckled and said, 'Ah, I's only joshin' with you boy. Go along with you, just shift it out of the way now. You got a cart coming to collect it?'

'Yes,' said West. 'Somebody'll be along directly.'

The mention of nitro had unnerved Johnny West and he felt a trickle of ice cold sweat running down from his armpits. Although brave enough in battle or when danger was imminent, he knew that if he and the others were detected in this activity, they would all hang. It was this prospect that filled him with dread, the thought of dying a felon's death on the gallows and not an honourable one by powder and shot.

Jed Taylor was trembling like an aspen leaf and West said to him, 'You can cut along now to get yourself a shot o' liquor, but mind you come straight to the hotel after. You can find it without me?'

'Oh surely, surely,' said Taylor, who was desperately anxious to seek out a saloon.

'You best not go on some big drinking spree,' said Johnny West coldly. 'You ain't fit to work tomorrow or you go missing or summat and I tell you now, I'm going to hunt you down and kill you like a mangy dog? We got that clear?'

The original plan for President Johnson's assassination had been formulated by Frank Mason and entailed a troop of Klansman riding into Terra Nova and gunning down the president and anybody else who happened to be standing near him. Via an intermediary, Edwin Stanton had rejected this plan out of hand. It still stung when he recalled the aftermath of Lincoln's death, when he had declared martial law and been about to seize the reins in Washington. But, of course, both Johnson, who had been vice president at that time and also Seward, the secretary of state, had survived to scotch Stanton's plans for power. He did not intend for the same thing to happen again. This time, due entirely to Johnson's hubris and desire to make an exhibition, all the main players would be crammed into one place, namely Terra Nova's civic hall. Stanton did not want to run the chance of any of those folk escaping out the back when the assassins opened fire. The attack on the government the previous year had been bungled, such a thing would not happen again.

So it was that Mason had come up with a new scheme, whereby eighty pounds of the deadliest explosive known to humanity would be secreted in the hall where the president was going to begin his grand tour. The stuff would be concealed beneath the stage where Johnson was to deliver his speech, and from what Johnny West had seen at that old mission station the quantity used would be more than enough to blow the entire hall to atoms, killing everybody within. There would be no mistakes on this occasion. If by some mischance there were any survivors, they would be gunned down by the five men stationed on the rooftops opposite the civic hall.

The fellow with the horse and cart, who had been engaged to meet the eastbound train when it pulled into the depot, finally turned up a good half-hour after Johnny West had unloaded the crates containing the acid and glycerine. The man in charge of the horse had a bulbous red nose and his speech was slightly slurred, suggesting to West that he suffered from the same weakness as Jed Taylor. 'You're late,' said West, staring at the man balefully, 'You should o' been here waiting for me.'

'Well, I'm here now.'

The little southerner could move with the all the speed of a striking rattler when he was roused. The owner of the cart had no sooner climbed down and set his foot on the ground, when Johnny West was on him, his hands grabbing hold of the man's shirtfront and almost lifting him up in the air by the material. He said, through gritted teeth, 'Do not get smart with me, my friend. It's apt to be the death of you, understand?'

'All right, all right,' said the other pacifically, 'No harm meant, I'm sure. I was delayed. I'm sorry.'

The smell of whiskey was sour on the man's breath and West said in disgust, 'Delayed by what, urgent

94

business in a saloon? Just get these crates loaded up and take 'em where I bid you. I'm going to sit along of you and give you directions.'

CHAPTER 6

Eliza Clancy was not best pleased to see the man whom her husband had thought fit to invite to stay. His appearance was against him to begin with, a bloody gash across his face and brown bloodstains all over the front of his shirt. He was dirty and unshaven too, to say nothing of smelling as though he hadn't had a bath in some long while. Learning that this disreputable-looking tramp was her brother-in-law did not increase her enthusiasm for his presence in the house. She had heard enough about this young man to know that he wasn't at all the sort she wished her children to associate with. Still and all, he was Grant's brother and so she greeted him civilly enough, saying, 'Why, Mister Clancy, I've heard a deal about you from my husband. You're very welcome.'

Brent was not at all deceived by these pleasant words, gauging quite correctly that here was a woman who would have him out of the house if he so much as breathed in the wrong direction. He said, 'I heard much about you too, ma'am,' which was a lie.

He'd assumed that his brother had a wife, but knew nothing definite about the matter. 'These must be your little ones, I'm guessing.'

The two small and unprepossessing children put Brent in mind of goblins from a fairy tale. Neither could have been above two or three years of age and the pair of them clung to their mother's skirts and peered at Clancy as though he were a strange animal. He smiled at them and said, 'Hidy!' in a cheerful voice, whereupon one of them burst into tears and the other buried his face in his mother's clothes, the better to block out the sight of him.

Grant said, 'You'll be wanting to wash and suchlike. You got shaving tackle?'

'I lost pretty much everything when I escaped from those people,' Brent reminded him. 'I got only what I stand up in.'

'I guess you'll have to use my razor, as well as my clothes.'

The evening meal was not a relaxing one for Brent. He was aware that his table manners lacked finesse and every time he wolfed down a mouthful without first chewing it, his sister-in-law shot him a look of gentle reproach, presumably for the bad example he was setting to her children. He was glad when the meal was over and he and his brother could retire to the garden to talk and smoke.

The garden was a delight for the senses, being filled with fragrant and colourful flowers. There was a little bench to rest on, the kind of thing that you might expect to find in some public park in a big city.

Once they were comfortably settled down, Brent said, 'I reckon you'll be wiring Washington and telling the president not to come?'

Grant shot him a quizzical look and said, 'Why would I do that?'

'Well, to save his life, maybe. There's some devilment afoot and it all seems to centre around your Main Street. I guess that Johnson's speaking in some building there.'

'He is.'

Brent Clancy was bewildered by his brother's calm and unruffled manner. He had supposed that the second Grant set his eyes upon the papers from the vanity case he would have been firing off telegrams to all and sundry, cancelling the presidential visit and hunting down any mischievous strangers who might be in town. He said, 'What then, you don't think what I showed you is a true bill?'

'Oh, as to that,' said Grant Clancy easily, 'I make no doubt that something's afoot. Concerns that blamed visit by the president too, I shouldn't wonder.' Seeing the puzzled look on his brother's face, the sheriff of Terra Nova laughed out loud. He continued, 'Listen, I cancel that big show and start kicking down doors looking for a band of assassins, what do you think will be the result? All those rats will scatter elsewhere and start some new plot. Maybe they'll be luckier next time and my brother won't rob them of some vital documents!' He chuckled. 'No, I aim to find the whole crew of 'em and arrest them. You ever had an abscess?

'Have I what?'

'Had an abscess, you know, like a carbuncle or large boil.'

'Sure,' said Brent, not seeing where this conversation was tending, 'But what's that got to do with the price of sugar?'

'You can squeeze an abscess clumsily and force the poison down deep into your flesh. Then you might end up with a dozen smaller boils, rather than the one big one. Or, you can let it get bigger and bigger, 'til there's a clear head to it. Then you lance it, jab a sharp blade in and drain out the pus.'

Understanding dawned and Brent looked at his brother with respect. He said, 'You mean you'll let these fellows carry on, so they think that they can continue with their murderous plans and then hope to catch the whole lot of them when the time is ripe?'

Grant nodded. 'I think so, yes.'

'It's the hell of a risk. These are dangerous characters.'

'I'm a dangerous character, too. So are you, if it comes to that. I'll do all right, I reckon, thanks to the warning you risked your life to carry to me.'

This was as close as his brother was likely to get to saying 'Thank you' and Brent thought that he had better be content with it. He had a sudden rush of wishing to make up for some of the disappointment that he had caused his mother, father and most likely his brother, too. He said, 'You want any help with this? Or can you and your deputies handle it without any assistance?'

'You know, I was kind of hoping that you'd ask that. You want in on this and it might go some way to making up for some of the capers you've been mixed up in since the end of the war.'

'You saying you do want my help?'

His brother shrugged nonchalantly. He surely was not about to ask more elaborately than he had already. He said, 'I reckon you're a handy fellow to have about if the going gets rough. I heard a heap about you over the last few years, never mind that we haven't met all that often. Some of it good, like what you did during the war and some not so good, like when you been on the scout. But I know that you can be relied upon in a fight and that you're scared of nothing. You want to help me, I won't say no.'

At about the time that the Clancy brothers were bidding fair towards growing closer than either of them could either recall ever having been before in their lives, Frank Mason was travelling towards them in the railroad train that he and his comrades had caught from the junction at Barker's Crossing. It was an integral part of Mason's nature that he rehearsed any projected action in which he was involved dozens of times before actually undertaking it. Some thought that this obsessive thought process was tantamount to an illness of the mind, but Frank Mason knew that it had saved his life in the past. His four companions were slumbering in the half-empty coach, which meant that they were not likely to distract his attention, for which Mason was mighty thankful.

President Johnson and his cavalcade were due to arrive in Terra Nova in forty-eight hours. That meant that the Klansmen would have the whole of the morrow to make their preparations and lay the mine that would, it was hoped, demolish the civic hall at which Johnson was scheduled to speak. Hiring a man who would mix up the nitro just before it was to be used had been Mason's idea. It would mean one more death; the man was a hopeless drunk who would need to be disposed of before Johnson hit town, but what was one more life when so much was at stake?

Jed Taylor would need to be killed as soon as he had prepared the explosives, but it was unlikely that anybody would miss him. He was not, after all, a citizen of Terra Nova. Killing the town's sheriff and a man who was probably related to him though, that would be a hard row to hoe without causing alarm in the town, which might in turn lead to the president cancelling his visit. Maybe, thought Mason, as he lay back against the seat with his eyes closed, it would prove possible to guy up Sheriff Clancy's death as an accident of some kind? Perhaps his house could burn down the night before President Johnson was expected in town. At this thought, Frank Mason smiled slightly and felt a good deal easier in his mind.

The day before the much-anticipated arrival of the President of the United States dawned bright and clear, with not the least wisp of cloud in the sky.

Grant Clancy had hired some extra men to sweep the street between the railroad depot and the hotel where Johnson would be staying. He was altogether determined that Terra Nova should be seen to best advantage. Word had been circulated that if anybody appeared on the streets drunk or even the worse for wear from imbibing liquor, then that person had best watch out, for he was liable to spend thirty days in the town's tiny little gaol cells. The sheriff saw this visit as something of a feather in his own cap and an implicit recognition by Washington that Terra Nova was an up and coming place, somewhere to watch in the future. And, as a man who had set his heart on becoming the mayor, once the city charter had been granted, it was in the sheriff's interests that the entire visit went smoothly and decorously.

In a run-down carriage house, in an alleyway off Main Street, Jed Taylor's life was fast slipping away, although of course he did not know that. He had, at Johnny West's urging, been early to bed the previous night and up bright and early at the crack of dawn, to prepare the eighty pounds of nitroglycerine, for which he was being paid such a large sum that he would be able to remain liquored up for the next year or so without working. West and Mason had been exceedingly generous in their offer of remuneration, for the simple reason that they had not the slightest intention of giving the man a single cent.

'I could surely do with just another little nip of the good stuff!' exclaimed Taylor, in a whining voice, 'I been working at this since first light.'

'You already had a shot o' rye,' Johnny West reminded him coldly, 'straight after you broke your fast before dawn. You'll not have another drop 'til this work is finished.'

'You're a hard man.'

'I'm a man who doesn't want to be blown sky high on account of some drunken bastard makes an error,' said West bluntly. 'How much longer will it take before you're done?'

'No more than an hour.'

'Well don't you hurry it none. If that stuff don't act according to plan, I'm going to come lookin' for you and I don't think you'd want that.'

The dusty carriage house was full of glass tubes, demijohns and carboys, all of which had been brought in and set up a week ago, following Taylor's instructions. The only thing that it had not proved possible to acquire and store beforehand had been the ice. Jed Taylor had assured those employing him that the nitro could be manufactured without cooling with ice, as long as a constant supply of running water could be laid on to remove the heat. Johnny West, for one, would be very pleased when the job was over and he could just kill this son of a bitch and then get on with the important matter of assassinating the president and then wresting control of the South back from the military government.

It was at first sight curious that although Grant Clancy had for the last few days been busy tidying up Terra Nova and attempting to conceal from sight any of its less savoury aspects, that he should insist that his own brother walk out of the house that day wearing the grimy and bloodstained clothes that he had on when he first fetched up at the sheriff's office the previous day. The reasoning was simple; Sheriff Clancy wanted his brother to stick out like the proverbial sore thumb, so that any of those who were seeking to take his life would immediately know that he was in town and looking for trouble.

The prospect of playing the part of a tethered goat did not precisely appeal to Brent Clancy, but he was bound to concede, in fairness to his brother, that the basic idea behind the trap was a sound one. All he had to do was walk about town as prominently as could be and hope that one of the Klansmen would recognize him and feel minded to either kill him on the spot or bring others to accomplish the task. It was unlikely that a murder would be committed out on the open street; these men still had to preserve their secrecy before they launched their bid to assassinate the president of the United States. Most likely, they would trail him and hope to catch him in a lonely spot, so that he could be disposed of with a dagger in the ribs or some similarly silent and inconspicuous way. Grant had explained that in India this was how they hunted tigers.

'See now,' he had told Brent, 'They tie up a goat or sheep and let it bleat away. Then the hunters set up a hide nearby and they wait. Wait 'til the noise of the goat or what have you attracts a tiger. Then, when the big cat shows up, bang! They have it.'

'Which sounds just fine and dandy,' said Brent Clancy, 'unless you happen to be the goat. Which, I suppose, you're asking me to be?'

'You want to get your own back on those boys, don't you? For killing your friends and causing you to leave your horse and other gear behind?'

'Don't try and buffalo me, Grant. This needs thinking on.'

'We ain't got a mort o' time, but I guess you know that.'

In the end, Brent Clancy agreed. It was true, he did wish to be revenged upon the men who had almost killed him, but there was more to it than that. Grant had been pretty decent about his turning up like that and had opened his home to his scapegrace brother without any hesitation. If he could do his respectable brother a good turn and help advance his prospects, well then it was only a fair exchange.

Brent said, 'You want me to look as rough and ready as can be and then go drawing attention to myself around town, is that right?'

'Me and my boys'll be behind you all the time. If anything will draw those fellows out the woodwork, this is it. They think you know all about whatever they got planned.'

'Ah, hell. Yeah, I'll do it. Won't be the first time in my life I played the goat!'

At that, Grant Clancy threw back his head and guffawed with laughter. He said, 'Ain't that the truth though?'

Brent, who could not recollect ever having heard

his staid and dignified brother laughing out loud in the whole course of his life, stared in amazement. When he had recovered himself, Grant said, 'Listen, you think you got the raw deal on family life, always having some wonderful big brother held up to you as an example of Godly behaviour and righteousness. Personally, I ain't a bit surprised you turned out like you did!'

In response to his brother's enquiring look, the sheriff of Terra Nova said slowly, 'You think I don't know how you had me and my doings rammed down your throat by our mother, God rest her soul, your whole life long? You think it's easy to be held up as a pattern of virtue, knowing your every move is being studied and admired? Well it ain't, I'll tell you that for nothing. It's a burden is what it is.'

'I never thought of it so.'

'I'm no saint, Brent. Just happens that I never took to liquor and I always feared the Lord. There's no virtue in it, that's how I am. I told Ma, you know. Told her to stop praising me up all the livelong day, but you think she'd listen? Like I say, I ain't the least bit surprised you cut loose as soon as you were able.'

While the Clancy brothers were having the first serious conversation they'd had since Brent became an adult, five men had booked into the Imperial Hotel, the grandest place to stay in Terra Nova. It was where President Johnson was to stay on the first night of his whistle-stop tour of the Union, which was due to begin the next day. The men had slept on the train and so just took the rooms, left their bags there and then went hunting for breakfast. They had not been such fools as to march into the hotel as a body of five men. Instead, they had entered at intervals and affected not to recognize each other. After depositing their luggage, which in every case amounted to little more than saddle-bags and portmanteaus, they made their way, one by one, to the disused carriage house where Jed Taylor was cooking up a large batch of nitro.

'How's it going, my friend?' asked Frank Mason amiably of the man he had hired.

'I'm quite finished, Mister Mason,' replied Taylor, obsequiously. 'Just let that stuff in those two carboys cool for a spell and there you have it. Eighty pounds of Black Hercules.'

'It looks a little murky,' said Mason dubiously. 'You sure it'll answer for our purposes?'

'Well, I ain't asked what your purposes are, you know,' said Taylor facetiously, 'But if you're after the devil of a bang, then it'll act alright.'

'And you say it's ready to use?'

'Soon as it's quite cool. Leave it for twelve hours and that's it.

'You'll be wanting your reward, I dare say?' asked Frank Mason, an almost imperceptible smile hovering at the corners of his mouth.

'What're you laughing at?' enquired Taylor uneasily. 'You're not minded to cheat me of what I got coming, I suppose?

'Not a bit of it, you'll get what's coming to you.'

While Mason was speaking, Johnny West had been moving casually behind the jumpy little drunkard and as he did so, he reached to a sheath that was affixed to the back of his belt. Nestling there in the small of his back was a razor-sharp bowie knife. Once he was behind Taylor and out of his line of sight, he drew the knife and then, in one swift movement, leaned forward, grabbed the man's hair, jerked back his head and then drew the blade briskly across the tautened flesh at the front of the Jed Taylor's throat. The bowie knife was sharp enough, but it was an awkward angle at which to cut and so West had to saw a little in order to get through the hard cartilage of the voice box. As soon as he had done so and the carotid artery was severed, blood sprayed out as though from a soda siphon.

West's action was greeted with cries of fury from the other men, who shouted things such as, 'Christ man, mind my jacket!' or 'What's wrong with you West, it's going everywhere!' The strong feelings expressed all seemed to be concerned with the mess created and the possibility of having their clothes stained. Not one of the six men present showed any emotion at the death of a fellow being in front of them.

There was little point in trying to hide the corpse and it was just rolled under a bench and an old tarpaulin thrown over it. If things went according to plan, there would be a number of deaths of far more consequence than the drunken engineer and it was unlikely that anybody would find Jed Taylor's body anyway until the half dozen Klansmen had been long-departed from the town. It was agreed to repair to the hotel for coffee and to make final preparations for the murders that would take place the following day. President Johnson was scheduled to arrive at the depot at four in the afternoon on the morrow, go to the hotel to freshen up and then deliver his great speech at eight in the evening. There was plenty of time to make the necessary dispositions.

Had they but known it, Mason and the rest of them missed Brent Clancy by a matter of seconds that morning. When they reached the hotel, the clerk said, 'Why, somebody was asking just now about any new folk recently arrived here. I wondered if he meant some others.'

'What did he look like?' asked Mason, 'Can you give a description?'

'Well now, he was a right scruffy looking type. Dirty clothes, blood down the front of his shirt. You'd surely know him if you saw him. Nasty cut running right up and down one cheek.'

Frank Mason did not reply but turned and walked straight out of the Imperial and looked up and down the street. He was unable to see anybody fitting the clerk's description, although he had little doubt that the man was the very same who had robbed him a few days back. The devil of it was that he was the only one in town who had got a good look at this Brent Clancy, up close. The others had only glimpsed him from a distance under the circumstances of the chase that had culminated in the wretch leaping aboard the Flyer. He would have to roam around town a bit now and try to run the boy to earth. Mind, with that scar on his face, he should be easy enough for anybody to recognize.

Under normal circumstances, it would probably have been a fairly simple and straightforward matter for Sheriff Clancy to ask around hotels and lodging houses in order to find out if there was a group of strangers in town. Of course, circumstances were anything but normal right now, with the President of the United States due to arrive the next day. A lot of people from surrounding farms were drifting into Terra Nova in the hope of catching a glimpse of Andrew Johnson. Not that he was enormously popular hereabouts, but after all, the president is the president and it is something to say that you've heard him speak or even just caught sight of him. The place was accordingly heaving with unfamiliar faces and the chances of picking out this or that stranger were exceedingly slim.

Setting his brother to wander the town and make himself conspicuous was the only scheme that Grant Clancy had been able to come up with at such short notice. After the conversation they had had that morning, he was asking if this whole thing was too much of a risk for Brent. It honestly seemed that the two of them might be able to form some kind of bond now and that was something that was quite unlooked for. It would be the hell of a thing if something were to befall Brent now, just when it seemed

110

that an old breach might be at the point of being healed.

As Brent paraded up and down Main Street and popped into various places where a man might stay the night, either Grant or one of his deputies was watching the passers-by to see if anybody was taking any special notice of the travel-stained young man. So far though, the only looks that Brent Clancy had attracted were those he would be apt to garner in any respectable and well-regulated town, which was to say slight distaste and disapproval. None of those looking at the man with the bloody clothing looked like they were planning to murder him.

By midday, Sheriff Clancy had decided that enough time had been spent on the exercise and told one of the deputies to tell his brother to follow a circuitous route to the office and meet him there. When Brent slipped into the sheriff's office, his brother was already waiting. He said, 'I think we've mined this reef to death. I don't doubt that those fellows who were chasing you are somewhere in town, but we'll not find them like this. You want to eat?'

'I'm pretty well starved.'

'Before we get something, I was wondering how you'd feel about carrying on lending me more of a hand, leastways 'til this blamed visit is over?'

'How so?'

'Why, as a deputy of course. I could give you a star and then we could set down here and try to work out what the game will be. If the two of us can't fathom out the case, then the Clancy family have fewer brains than I'd always thought.'

'I don't see that there's much to think over,' said Brent. 'I'd say that somebody, most like those men who were after me, are planning to kill the president. Either they'll blow him up or they'll start shooting from the rooftops, but it's too much of a coincidence, that map and all.'

'I read it the same way. But short of calling in the army, I'm not sure what I can do to guard against every type of mischief. They might have a mine laid at the railway depot already or be planning to shoot at the president as he speaks at the civic hall or a hundred other things. There's only so much I can do. I only have four deputies, if you'll believe it.'

'Well, I reckon you've got five, if you mean what you say about wanting to sign me up.'

'I'm right glad to hear it. Once I've sworn you in, I'll trouble you to check out some of those lines on that map, the ones that look like lines of fire. It might help us to figure out if some of those people who are in on this are fixing for to start shooting at the president from rooftops or something of the sort. Fine reputation that'll give the town! Go down in history as the place where the president was shot by assassins.'

Although Grant was speaking lightly, it was plain that he was seriously disturbed about what might be about to happen in Terra Nova. When some terrible thing in the law-breaking way occurs somewhere, the local police or sheriff usually gets the blame and is criticised for lack of vigilance. Quite apart from any objective compassion and concern for the welfare of President Johnson, it would certainly be a blow to Grant Clancy's political ambitions in Terra Nova, should any harm befall him while he was in town.

CHAPTER 7

When he went to his bed that evening, Brent Clancy felt more at ease with himself and his life than he had since the beginning of the war. He and his brother were starting to get to know each other and it turned out that maybe Grant was not such an out and out stiff'un as Brent had always supposed. Lordy, they were even working alongside each other; something that a few days ago would have seemed to Brent like some kind of extravagant fantasy. Even Eliza and her children had unbent towards him. When she heard that her husband had appointed Brent as a temporary deputy, she knew that her brother-in-law must be a more trustworthy and reliable individual than she had thought. That was enough for her to give the fellow the benefit of the doubt. This softened attitude towards Brent had been picked up by her children, who consented to allow their uncle to read them a story at bedtime. All in all, the evening had been the pleasantest that Brent could recollect since the war had ended.

Brent was awoken in the middle of the night by a strange cracking sound. He listened in the darkness to the creaking and cracking, until he was sure that it was not the aftermath of some disturbing dream. Then he opened his eyes and discovered that the darkness was not as absolute as might have been expected. From outside the window he could see an eerie and flickering glow. It took but the merest fraction of a second for him to combine the wavering light with the crackling sound and for Clancy to realize that the house was on fire. He leapt from the bed and rushed over to the door, grabbing at the brass handle and finding that it was practically red hot. Nevertheless, he grasped it and opened the door, to be greeted by a roaring wall of flame.

There would have been no purpose in Clancy trying to walk through the furnace that the corridor outside his room had become. There was mischief afoot, of that he had no doubt. For this reason, he snatched up the pistol lying on the table by the bed and then pulled on his jacket. For want of night attire, he had been sleeping in his britches and so he looked decent enough. The window was open and Clancy scrambled through it.

The drop to the ground below was not a considerable one, Clancy thought that by hanging from the ledge and reducing the distance to the ground a little, he could manage it without any serious injury. What shocked him was the brightness from the next window to his, where the curtains had evidently taken fire and were now sending out sparks into the night. The whole house must be ablaze! It was a wonder that none of the neighbours had yet noticed, which even as he hung from the windowsill struck Clancy as a strange and significant circumstance. The fall into the garden winded him, but he did not, as he had feared, break or even sprain either of his ankles. As soon as he landed, he sprang to his feet, but saw at once that the case was hopeless.

It was only the fact that he had been sleeping in the spare bedroom that had saved Brent Clancy's life. It was jutting out a little from the rest of the upper storey and so was slightly removed from the fire below. The whole lower floor of the house was a raging inferno and the upper floor too, with the sole exception of the corner of the house where his room had been, was also burning fiercely. Nobody could have survived such a holocaust. Despite this pessimistic conviction, Clancy raced around to the back door of the house, which let on to the garden. The glass in this was shattered, as were all the windows; allowing a powerful draught of air to enter the house and feed the flames. Entering through that way would simply end in him being burned to a crisp and so he went haring round the side of the house to see if the front door facing the street would be any better. It was not. The hallway, or what could be glimpsed of it through the flames, was almost entirely consumed, as was the staircase. It was as he stood there, debating in his mind how he could make a rescue attempt, that there came a colossal, splintering crash and a sudden surge of fire from the windows. The floor of the upper storey of the house had crashed down into the ground floor. Any faint hope that somebody might be left alive was now extinguished. Clancy just stood there, his eyes blinded by tears. It was only at this point that the first of the neighbours appeared on the scene.

'Lord a mercy,' said the middle-aged man who hurried up, evidently having thrown a coat over his nightshirt. 'What a fearful thing. Did everybody get out safely, would you know?'

The roar of the internal collapse of the Clancy family's home had seemingly woken others, for in ones and twos, others drifted to the roadway outside the burning house. They muttered things like, 'Terrible, terrible!' and 'Did the children get out safely?' For his part, Brent could not speak. He just stood there dumbly, hoping that the children had died swiftly of smoke inhalation, rather than suffering the agony of being burned alive. One of the men living nearby was looking hard at Clancy in the glare of the flames and at length came over to him and said in a sharp, suspicious voice, 'I don't mind that you live hereabouts. What brings you here at such a time?'

Some of those who were watching the fire came over to see what answer Clancy would make to this challenge. It was clear enough to him that he was suspicioned of starting the fire. He said, 'My name's Brent Clancy. I'm the sheriff's brother.'

Because he had no time for fooling around and was in any case struck all of a heap by the death of his brother and his family, Clancy decided to cut all this short at once. He did so by drawing attention to the star that his brother had pinned to his jacket less than twelve hours ago. He said, 'Case none of you have noticed, I'm a deputy and if anybody's going to be asking questions, that'll be me. Everybody understand that?' It seemed that they did, for there were no more questions, although Clancy received many sidelong glances. He looked around the gathering crowd and said, 'Anybody see or hear anything? Before the fire, I mean.'

Apparently, nothing had been heard or seen and the first that anybody present had known of the matter was the crash of the inside of the sheriff's house collapsing in on itself. Clancy said, 'Does this town run to a fire brigade?'

'There's a bunch of volunteers. You want I should rouse 'em?'

'What do you think?' asked Clancy sarcastically, 'You reckon that would be a smart move?'

'I'll run over and knock on a few doors.'

It took the better part of an hour for the fire crew to arrive, by which time the wooden-framed house was in the last stages of collapse. The fire engine was no more than a large tank of water, which had to be pumped by two men operating a mechanism that resembled a seesaw. They sprayed water at the house, which damped down the flames a little, while one of the men began poking around the garden. After a spell, the man who it seemed was in charge of the town's fire crew came over to where Clancy was standing. He had been directed there by some of the men standing around. Word had spread that this scruffy young stranger was apparently a deputy, which made him the nearest thing to a representative of authority in the vicinity. Most of the people who had come out to watch somebody's house burn down were returning to their homes now. They had fulfilled their civic duty by sending for the fire engine and commiserating with the only survivor of the blaze and, it now being nigh on three in the morning, wished only to snuggle down again in their beds. The fireman said, 'Pardon me for asking, but they say you're a lawman.'

It was an extraordinary turnabout for Brent to find himself in such a character, but he had to admit the truth of the man's tentative enquiry. He said, 'I reckon so. Leastways, I'm a deputy and the sheriff is dead. How can I help?'

'Thought you might care to see what we found round the side of yon house,' said the man, his face grim. 'Looks to me like that fire weren't no accident.'

'The hell you talking about?' asked Clancy roughly, 'What have you found?'

'Come along of me and I'll show you.'

The house was all but burned out now. It had been a long, dry summer and the wooden building had flared up like a tinderbox, but with the fuel exhausted and the water sprayed on the smouldering remains by the firemen, it would be only an hour or so before the flames died down entirely. Clancy followed the man round to a side window and watched silently as he picked up two earthenware flagons. He handed one to Clancy, saying, 'Smell that!' There was the reek of lamp oil.

'You reckon as somebody used oil to get a fire going?' asked Clancy, hardly able to believe that any human being would do such a wicked thing, 'Is that the only thing you come across?'

'There's this as well, though I ain't precisely sure what to make of it.' The man bent down and took from a flowerbed a sheet of brown paper, as large as a newspaper. He held it out for Clancy's inspection. The paper was sticky and there were small fragments of glass stuck to it. 'What do you make of it?'

Clancy knew very well what to make of it and he felt fury rising within him so fiercely that for a moment he thought he would choke. Then he recollected himself and said quietly, 'You don't know what this signifies? But then, why should you? It's an old trick used by men breaking into property. They smear a pint or two of treacle all over a window and then press brown paper on top of it. Then, they break the window. All the noise when you break a window comes from the glass falling everywhere. The actual breaking itself just makes a muffled crack. Do that at night and you can enter a home, store, bank, what have you, nice and quiet. Just pull off the paper and it takes all the glass with it.'

'Why, you don't say so? You surely know your stuff, deputy. I can leave all this with you then?'

Clancy saw no advantage to letting the man know that knowledge of this particular method of burglary dated back to an abortive raid that he and another had attempted on a bank, one dark night. He limited himself to saying quietly, 'I'll engage to handle everything from here on in.'

Events were moving at such a breakneck speed that Clancy felt dizzy. He could not rid his mind of the image of those little ones to whom he had read a story just a few hours since. They and their mother and his own brother, all dead. What kind of men would do an atrocious thing like that, killing a woman and children in that way? Deep in his heart, he already knew the answer to that. These were members of the same band who had pursued him here. It was all tied up with President Johnson's visit.

There was no prospect at all of his being able to sleep any more that night, even had he a bed, and so Clancy thought he'd go down to his brother's office and see what could be done in preparation for the big day that would soon be dawning. Although he wasn't at all bothered about some politician from Washington being murdered, those planning this crime were without doubt the same men who had so cruelly massacred his brother and his family. Clancy's personal desire for vengeance happened to coincide with the requirements of law and order. He would be able to hunt down and kill those dogs quite legally.

Four hours later, Grant Clancy's deputies arrived at the sheriff's office. Their boss had impressed upon them most forcibly that this was an important day and that, as he put it, all hands were needed on deck. The first two men to reach the office found the young man who had been introduced to them the day before as Sheriff Clancy's brother. This fellow was sitting at the boss's desk, looking through the paperwork there as though he was in charge.

A single, small pane of glass was missing from the street door, which led the two deputies to suppose that the man sitting at the sheriff's desk had forced an entry to the office. Before they had a chance to express their outrage at this, he apprised them of Grant's death and asked which of the deputies was now in charge, until a new sheriff was appointed. It appeared that neither of the men knew the answer to this and nor did the other two men when they fetched up a quarter-hour later.

'Two of you know that my brother swore me in yesterday afternoon,' said Clancy, 'And I'm now a legally appointed deputy. I don't aim for to tread on anybody's toes, but I'll be tracking down the men who murdered my brother and his wife and little'uns. If none o' you fellows is in charge now, then you can deal with matters as you see fit. I know what my brother planned this day and I'll carry out his wishes as best I'm able.' Which the four men in the office interpreted, quite correctly, to mean, 'I'll do as I please and don't care a damn what the rest of you do; just don't get crosswise to me!'

The longest-serving of the four deputies, Tom Parker, who had just turned forty, said, 'I'll wire to the County Seat and let 'em know what's happened. You reckon as we should stop old Andrew Johnson coming to town?'

'No,' said Clancy very firmly. 'First off, it's not what my brother wanted and secondly, I want to catch those as killed him. If they're going after the president, then that gives me a chance to catch them.'

Brent might have been younger than all of them, but there was something about him that they all recognized, a determination to achieve his purpose no matter how much blood was shed. Not one of them wanted to try conclusions with this man. Parker, who felt that if anybody should be in charge now that Grant was seemingly deceased it should probably be him, said, 'Your brother was to meet the president at the depot when he arrives. I reckon as I should take over that duty, if nobody objects.' There were no objections.

From what he'd seen yesterday, when clambering over the rooftops opposite the civic hall, Clancy had come to the conclusion that the sketch map that he had acquired when taking down the stage lately did indeed show lines of fire and that whatever else was going to happen this day, men with rifles would be overlooking the front of the place where President Johnson was speaking. These sharpshooters were likely to be a back-up for a mine designed to destroy the civic hall completely. That too seemed obvious from the description of the building being blown up, which had also been in the vanity case he had lifted.

From Brent Clancy's perspective, the matter could hardly be simpler. Just as he had made his peace with his elder brother and was perhaps on the point of settling down a little, it had all been snatched away from him by an act of cold-blooded murder. Not only that, but the killings of the children and their mother meant there was a need for vengeance. He alone was in a position to set things straight and so it was upon him that the duty devolved.

Johnny West was a supremely ruthless and efficient killer, although an exceedingly slapdash and untidy one into the bargain. He had gained a savage and unholy joy from burning down a lawman's house the night before, but had, in his excitement, left the evidence of the crime scattered about in the garden, quite forgetting that the deaths were supposed to appear accidental. That was the problem with using West, you never quite knew how he would behave or what he would do when the killing lust was upon him. Nobody knew this better than Frank Mason, who sometimes wondered if Johnny West were not becoming more of a liability than an asset. Still, for now, there was certainly a place in the Great Enterprise for a man of such peculiarly useful talents.

West had three special hatreds, which were Yankees, lawmen and coloured folks, roughly in that order. As a merciless killer for the Ku Klux Klan, these deep-seated prejudices came in very useful, as did a native cunning and intelligence that enabled the man to see paths through a problem when other and more acute minds remained baffled. Johnny West had never set eyes upon Brent Clancy and had been given only the sketchiest description of the fellow, but it was enough for him to be able to track the man down, when the others who had actually seen Clancy had been unable to do so. He had simply reasoned that if, as was strongly suspected, the fellow was related to the man whose family West had slaughtered a few hours earlier, then he might reasonably be expected to be seeking vengeance. Where would be the most logical place for him to fetch up? Why, the office of his murdered relative of course!

Armed only with the knowledge that the boy he was hunting was a fresh-faced fellow of about twenty years of age, with jet black hair and a scar on his cheek, Johnny West wandered down in the direction of the sheriff's office a few hours after burning down the house. He saw at once, as he sauntered past, that somebody was already sitting in there, with a lamp burning, at six in the morning. This was in itself curious, but he kept on walking, not wishing to draw undue attention to himself. When the deputies began arriving an hour later, there were more people up and about; store-owners pulling up their shutters and blinds, men delivering goods and a few horses and carts heading over to the depot. After passing and repassing the office, glancing through the window each time in the most natural and casual fashion, West established that there was a very young man sitting in the office, apparently explaining out a case to the deputies he had seen coming to the office. This young man had black hair and he would have taken oath that it was the very person for whom Mason and the others had been hunting in vain.

By lingering on the opposite side of the road, West

was able to observe the young man in whom he was interested leaving the office. He noted, to his surprise, that he was sporting a tin star. This young man's hair was lustrous, almost blue-black, and it had been the colour of his hair that had most been remarked upon by those who had seen him in the flesh. That, combined with the fact that he could see the bloody gash on his face that had been talked of, told Johnny West that without the shadow of a doubt this was the man whom Mason wished to see killed before President Johnson arrived in town. He set off after the man, meaning to kill him quietly, just as soon as the opportunity presented itself.

Few men are able to survive four years of bitter, bloody war, followed by a year and a half of living as an outlaw, without acquiring a sixth sense for danger. Brent Clancy had a finely honed instinct that warned him of any threat to his life. He couldn't have explained this to others, it was just something that he knew, as surely as he could feel when rain was coming or that there would be a frost in the night. As he left his late brother's office that morning, he knew without the shadow of a doubt that somebody nearby meant him ill. He did nothing so obvious as to peer over his shoulder or start running. Instead, he moved at a leisurely pace down Main Street, in the direction of the railroad depot. Then, starting as though he had recollected something, he turned on his heel and began hurrying back towards the sheriff's office.

Taken aback at the sight of his quarry bearing

down on him, Johnny West was momentarily flustered and he halted in his tracks and began taking a great interest in the nearest store front. It was this slight hesitation that betrayed him and marked him out to Clancy as the one who had been following him. Brent Clancy walked past without giving any outwards show of noticing anything or anybody, but merely walked on briskly, like a man who is late for some pressing engagement. Emboldened by this, West resumed his pursuit, congratulating himself on being a pretty sharp operator when it came to hunting men. He saw the man ahead duck into the space between two buildings and speeded up his pace. Once they were out of sight of others, he could kill this troublesome boy and that would be one fewer thing for he and his friends to concern themselves about on this most important of days.

So confident was Johnny West of having the drop on the fellow he was following that he turned the corner into the alley without even pausing to peep round and ensure that everything was as he expected. Had he done so, he might not have been taken by surprise when two hands shot out. One grabbed his belt and the other his shirt-front. He was then swung round unceremoniously and slammed into the nearby brick wall. Before he had recovered from this surprising turn of events, his pistol was plucked from its holster and hurled down the alleyway. He had no time to draw breath or recover from the unusual feeling of having been utterly overwhelmed and taken wholly unawares when there was the sharp click of a pistol being cocked and he felt the cold metal of a gun barrel being jammed painfully under his jaw. It was done in such a way that he was unable to pull free because the barrel was hooked into the soft flesh beneath his chin and pressed against his jawbone. A soft but deadly voice enquired, 'I wonder what you've been up to, you son of a bitch. You stink of lamp oil and the smell of burning, you know that?'

It was by no means the first tight squeeze in which West had found himself and although matters had taken an unlooked-for turn, that did not mean that he was about to stick his head in a noose by making any damaging admissions. Nor was there any purpose in trying to wriggle free of the trap in which he now found himself. His enemy's weapon was cocked and he was unable to move his head by the least fraction of an inch. Instead, Johnny West let his body relax a little, as though in despair and at the same time moved his hand casually to the small of his back, as though trying to ease the pain from the awkward pose he was in. Then he drew the bowie knife that nestled at the back of his belt and brought it out swiftly, meaning to gut like a fish the man holding him.

Instead of the deep, slashing strike he intended, West only managed to jab feebly at the man holding him at such a tricky angle. It was, however, enough to make the other man loosen his grip a little in shock at the sudden pain. In a flash, West had squirmed free and shot off into the busy thoroughfare. Clancy drew his gun and set off in pursuit, but his erstwhile prisoner had too much of a lead on him. Besides which, Brent was not at all inclined to run until he had examined the harm that might have been wrought to his belly. There was no point in sprinting off down the road only for his intestines to start slopping out over the roadway.

By a miracle, the knife had wrought him no harm at all. The strength of the thrust had been largely intercepted by the stout leather belt around his waist. It had been a close run thing though, a quarter-inch lower and he would be lying in the alleyway right now, watching his life's blood running out into the dirt. He'd have the devil of a bruise to show for it, but the leather had stopped the blade from piercing his vitals and that was something to be thankful for. It had just penetrated the leather, leaving a superficial cut on his stomach. It was little more than a scratch though, certainly not sufficient to impair Clancy's efficiency in carrying out his self-appointed task that day.

Clancy knew now that the man who had run off after trying to kill him was the one who had burned down his brother's house and killed the entire family. Who else in that town would both reek of oil and smoke and also have a desire to follow him? More to the point, he had the best possible description now to give to hotel owners or lodging house keepers. Where he was, then the others would be close at hand. With some luck, he would be able to settle accounts for his brother's murder and prevent anything untoward happening to President Johnson, which he himself didn't care much about, but had been important to Grant. It would be an act of honour to his brother's memory to thwart whatever plan those boys had in mind for this day.

'I tell you, he was wearing a star,' said Johnny West, 'Sure as I'm standing here.'

'Then it can't be the one I was looking for,' replied Mason, 'He can't have changed from road agent to deputy in a matter of hours.'

'If he was related to that dead sheriff, he might,' observed one of the others, 'Could have sworn him in. They say blood's thicker than water.'

'It's too late to fret over,' said Frank Mason. 'If it is the same man as robbed me, then he can't do anything to stop us now. When we spring our mine, maybe he'll be standing by and guarding Johnson.'

'You don't reckon as we should change tack?' asked another of the men lounging around the hotel room.

'Not a bit of it. We'll get the gear stowed 'neath the stage and carry on. Anybody sees that boy, they can kill him, nice and quiet if they can. Otherwise, it makes no odds. Long as Stanton holds up his end o' the bargain, that boy can yap as much as he likes.'

The citizens of Terra Nova were proud of their civic hall, which was used for everything from dances and concerts to political meetings and speeches by men of the local council. It had a large stage, sufficient to accommodate an orchestra and enough space for hundreds of people to stand in the body of the hall. This morning, the place was a veritable hive of industry, with people climbing ladders to hang bunting and others sweeping the floor and removing the wooden chairs, to make more room, so that everybody who wished to do so could have a peek at the president. There was rumoured to be an entire coach full of reporters accompanying the president on his tour and Terra Nova was determined to present itself to best advantage.

So rapidly had Terra Nova expanded that the town's services had been unable to keep pace. One sheriff and four deputies were nowhere near adequate to maintain order and had it not been for the fact that the majority of the population were decent and law-abiding, things could have come to a crisis before this day. As it was, with three deputies out patrolling the streets, only one could be spared to check that everything was as it should be at the civic hall. This man, Tom Parker, was wandering around at the back of the stage when there came a rap on the back door of the hall, which let out onto an empty lot. He opened the door and was confronted by four men who had a load on a hand barrow. One of them said, 'We've to set this down here.' He consulted a sheet of paper and continued, 'Says we got to put it in the space beneath the stage. See, there's a little door over yonder that gives access.'

Parker saw nothing strange about the idea; people had been coming and going all morning with various deliveries and so on. He said, 'I'll check with the

131

organiser. You fellows wait here a moment.' There was nobody else at back of the stage at that moment and so when Parker turned to hunt out the man in charge of the arrangements for this evening's meeting and the person who had told him about the delivery leapt on his back and knocked him to the floor, there was nobody to see what was happening. While Johnny West killed the deputy, by the simple expedient of sticking his knife in Parker's chest, one of the others opened the little door giving on to the storage space beneath the stage and swiftly bundled the bloody corpse out of sight, pushing it down the short flight of steps into the darkness, among the boxes and barrels stashed out of the way there. The others lifted one of the heavy carboys off the barrow and, very carefully, carried it under the stage, setting it down next to the external wall. With luck, nobody would suspect that any harm had befallen the deputy. Maybe they would just think that he had wandered off for a drink or something.

CHAPTER 8

Sitting alone in his study, Edwin Stanton felt like a chess player about to bring off a fantastically elegant checkmate in just one more move. Andrew Johnson had few supporters and Stanton had subtly canvassed all the important political and military figures in Washington, sounding them out about their loyalty to the president. Almost to a man, they were willing to switch their allegiance if circumstances warranted it. Stanton talked delicately of the precarious position in which Johnson now found himself, hinting at the possibility of impeachment, with all the uncertainty that such a development would bring and the paralysis that would be brought to the government if matters ever reached that far. He had personal assurances from General Grant that the army would follow Stanton's orders to withdraw from the South and he had also spoken to the most eminent constitutional lawyer in the country and found that his scheme of suspending the constitution was quite legal, as long as certain conditions were met. If the men from the Klan fulfilled their part of the bargain then by nightfall Edwin Stanton would be virtually a dictator, in complete and utter control of the northern states of America and answerable only to his own conscience.

Nobody seemed to have noticed the disappearance of Tom Parker; there was simply too much going on in the civic hall for one man's absence to be a matter of remark. The two heavy carboys, each weighing a little over forty pounds, had been gently manoeuvred into place, as far as could be judged, right beneath the lectern at which the president would be standing. They would erupt like volcanoes, smashing the entire building to fragments, as effectively as a similar quantity of liquid had demolished that old mission station. Frank Mason, who knew something of such matters, unreeled a spool of safety fuse and ran it from one of the huge glass vessels to the outer wooden wall of the cellar-like space in which they were working. He pushed one end of the fuse out through a little hole, where he had knocked out a knot hole in a plank, so that it protruded for a foot or so. At the other end, right on top of one of the carboys, he attached a flask of black powder.

Walking the streets in hope of coming across the man who had tried to knife him did not seem to Clancy a good use of his time and energy. Instead, armed now with a highly detailed and specific description of the man whom he was perfectly certain had murdered his brother and his family, he resolved to visit some hotels. He struck lucky on the first he tried, the smartest one in town.

'Why yes,' said the clerk at the counter of the Imperial, 'Strikes me that you are talking of a fellow who booked in yesterday morning. He hooked up with some friends who had already arrived here.'

'I'd like to see their rooms, if you please.'

'Well, I suppose it will be all right,' said the fellow dubiously, 'The manager ain't here just now, but if you'd care to come back in an hour or so. . . .'

'This is a matter of life and death,' said Clancy curtly, 'You frustrate my purpose and you'll answer for it in court.'

That did the trick and seeing as the man before him was, by all appearances, a genuine deputy sheriff, the clerk led him up to the rooms occupied by the seven men. There was nothing of interest in the rooms though, notwithstanding that they had been booked for the week and cash paid upfront. Clancy toyed briefly with the idea of staying there and staging an ambush, but time was running precious short. He knew from the conversation with the other deputies that one of them was to be stationed permanently at the civic hall, so there was no point in going there. He decided to go down to the depot instead, the germ of an idea beginning to ferment in his mind. Before that though, he wished to take a look at a building that he had noticed earlier, the new bank. He smiled involuntarily at the idea of his scouting out a bank now, not with a view to robbing it but rather as a deputy, desirous of preventing the commission of a felony. You surely never knew how things were going to turn out in this world!

As he strode down Main Street towards the railroad depot, Clancy's brain was working furiously. He'd no idea how it was to be done, but from all that he was able to comprehend from those papers, the focus for any mischief was to be the civic hall. That's where all the lines of fire were drawn and unless he and his brother had been greatly mistaken, some kind of explosion was planned there as well. What if the president never went anywhere near the civic hall though? Suppose that he could be diverted away from the place on some pretext? That would surely have the effect of luring those skunks into the open and forcing them to reveal themselves. But what could he say to President Johnson to cause him to change his plans?

By the time he had reached the depot, Clancy's plan had assumed solid form. It was a scheme that would flush those assassins from hiding and give him a chance to take them. His plan seemed, at least to him, mighty thin, but for want of any better this would be what he would go with. It all depended upon just how proud of himself the president was.

It was no secret that President Johnson was as vain as a peacock. What Clancy had decided was that he would approach the president in his official capacity as deputy sheriff and tell him that the civic hall was too small and that so many people were desperately anxious to see him that it would be fairer for the folk in the town if he were to give his speech in the open. This should flatter the man. If he could persuade the president, then there would be no reason at all for Johnson to set foot in the civic hall. He could go straight from the Imperial Hotel to the bank and anybody wishing to kill him would be compelled to come right into the open.

The First National Bank of Illinois was the latest addition to what was fast becoming Terra Nova's business district. A handsome and imposing brick-built structure, it was covered in gleaming white stucco. The paintwork around the windows and doors was a pleasing shade of green and, as an architectural flourish, wrought iron balconies had been incorporated into the front and at the side on the upper floor. What especially interested Brent Clancy was that the balcony at the side overlooked an empty lot, because this was now the furthest extent of the offices and stores of Main Street. If the president gave his speech from this balcony, then the whole town would be able to listen to him. More to the point, from Clancy's point of view, anybody wishing to launch an attack upon the president would be obliged to show himself. Shooting at him with a rifle would not be an attractive option for there were no buildings facing the balcony. With luck, he could bring them out into the open and this would give him the chance to nail the bastard who had killed his brother.

There would be a fair crowd of folk at the depot in a few hours, awaiting the arrival of President

Johnson's special train. Clancy wanted to ensure that no attempt would be made on anybody's life actually at the depot. If there were to be an explosion there, it would be a fearful business. The manager of the place though assured him that nothing was out of the ordinary. He said, 'I reckon me or the fellows would have noticed anything untoward. It's just like a regular day though, bar this here "special" that's coming through in a couple of hours.'

For the next few hours, Clancy prowled the town like a restless and angry tiger. He knew that the man who had killed his brother and tried to kill him was still on the loose, but wherever he was, he was keeping his head down. Just as well for him, for Clancy knew that the next time they encountered each other, one of them was sure to die.

In the course of the brief conversation that he had had with him earlier that morning, Tom Parker had struck Clancy as the sort of plodding stickler for rules who would be hard to shift from what he saw as the 'official' course of action. Clancy had prepared various arguments that he hoped would suffice to persuade the older man to deviate from the planned itinerary for the president's stay in Terra Nova. When he got to the depot at about half past three though, there was no sign of Parker. When it lacked five minutes to the hour and there was still no indication that Parker was likely to be taking part in the reception, Clancy breathed a little easier. Word received from down the line, via the telegraph, suggested that the special train was running a few minutes late.

Brent took the opportunity to approach the group of smartly dressed councilmen who were waiting to greet President Johnson. They proved easier to deal with than he had thought likely. Having approached the leader of the council, Clancy said respectfully, 'Sir, I'm right sorry to trouble you. I'm the brother of your late sheriff. . . .'

'Late sheriff?' asked the elderly man in some bewilderment. 'I haven't the pleasure of understanding you, young man.'

'My brother Grant was killed last night. His house burned down. He swore me in as a deputy though, there's a couple of the other deputies can vouch for me.'

'That's terrible, just terrible. I heard there'd been a fire, but I didn't know . . . I'm sorry for your loss. And ours. Your brother was a fine man.'

'He laid a charge upon me before he died, in a manner of speaking. It relates to the president.'

The councilmen were all looking at Clancy now and he wondered what they made of him. Not much, most likely. He said, 'My brother was uneasy about President Johnson speaking in an enclosed space. He wanted the arrangement changed, so that the president addresses the town not in the civic hall, but rather from the balcony in the new bank building, the one overlooking the vacant lot.' Brent Clancy had never read, nor even heard of Machiavelli, but he was certainly following that writer's dictum that when the end is lawful, then this justifies the means. He felt a little bad about attributing his plan to his dead brother, but felt that the idea would carry more weight with the council if they thought that it came from Grant Clancy, rather than his disreputable-looking young brother.

'Are you saying that your brother had some apprehension of harm befalling the president while he was in the town?' asked one of the councilmen.

'I am, sir,' replied Clancy truthfully. 'It was greatly on his mind yesterday.'

The last thing anybody wished was for something to happen to the president in the course of his stay in town. After a brief consultation among themselves, the leader of the council said to Clancy, 'If Sheriff Clancy truly thought that having President Johnson speak outside, rather than in the hall, was for the best, then I can see no objection to adopting that course of action.'

'Perhaps if we told the president that we are doing this because so many folk are desirous of seeing him, it might make him less inclined to cancel his engagement entirely?'

'Was that you brother's idea, son, or your own?'

'Mine, sir.'

'Well, it's sound enough.'

So it was that when ten minutes later the special pulled into the depot, Clancy was able to stand on the sidelines, watching the crowd intently, alert for any sign of hostility towards the president.

The presidential party, including Secretary of State Seward and various other dignitaries, made their way on foot down Main Street to the Imperial

Hotel, where they were scheduled to rest up for a few hours until the time came for Johnson's great speech about preserving the Union, by which he meant, of course, his own presidency. He was by no means displeased to be told that so great was the eagerness to hear him speak that the civic hall was quite inadequate for the purpose. Hadn't he said all along that ordinary people were the ones with the brains to recognize a good thing when they saw it? Let those fools in Washington see how popular he was and gnaw their tongues in impotent fury, he would show them.

The first intimation that Mason and the others had that their plan was in jeopardy came from Johnny West. Frank Mason and his four companions were seated peaceably in an eating house, drinking coffee and generally keeping out of the way while the president arrived in town and settled in. After Johnny West's run-in with the sheriff's brother, it was felt that the less that the conspirators showed themselves on the public streets, the less chance was there of their scheme miscarrying because of some private act of vengeance from the hot-headed young road agent. When West appeared, at about five, three hours before President Johnson was giving his speech, the five men in the eating house were feeling as relaxed as you like. Nothing could go wrong now and the game was all but over. The short length of fuse protruding from the wall of the civic hall needed only to be ignited and then, four minutes later, there would be the loudest sound ever heard in this town.

As soon as West walked through the door, it was

141

plain that he was greatly perturbed in his mind. He walked straight over to Mason and said in a low voice, 'We got a big, big problem. Johnson ain't speaking at the hall. Not going near nor by the place, neither.'

'What the Deuce are you talking about?' asked Mason, a feeling of dread gripping him. 'He's here alright, saw him through the window, walking down the street with his men. What d'you mean, he's not going to speak?'

'He's a goin' for to speak, just not at that hall. He's addressing the crowd from some balcony, down the way.'

'How sure are you?'

'Certain sure. It's the theme of general conversation on the street. Something 'bout the civic hall being too small.'

For a few seconds, all six of them looked at each other wordlessly, seeing the ruination of all their hopes. Then Mason said harshly, 'Well then, we'll need to try another way, won't we?'

'Like what?' asked one of the men sitting at the table.

'First off is where we need to see where this speech is being given now,' said Frank Mason. Turning to West he asked, 'You know where it's happening?'

'Sure.'

'Then, gentlemen,' said Mason, 'We have only a few hours to prepare.' He got to his feet and the others followed suit. The prospect of failure was not only an appalling one to them, meaning as it did, the continued and oppressive military occupation of the southern states by the Union army, it also presented them with the very real possibility that their recent crimes might be brought home to them, with fatal consequences.

Clancy was ready for any desperate action, knowing that once their plans had been upset, the men who had lately been on his tail would stick at nought. The stakes that such men were playing for were so high that they surely knew that their lives would be forfeit if they failed. One only had to look at the way that Mary Surrat, whose only crime had been renting a room to the man who had shot Abraham Lincoln, had been hanged. The men in the present case had encompassed the death of the president and worked actively to bring it about. They had nothing to lose now. Brent Clancy was musing along these lines while perched on the very roof of the civic hall. He had figured that whatever plans had been made must feature either this place or the Imperial Hotel. From his vantage point, Clancy was able to watch both locations and so spotted immediately when the man who had stabbed him earlier that day came into view below, accompanied by five other men. One of these was the man whose watch and papers Clancy had stolen when he knocked over the stage to Indian Falls. Everything was falling neatly into place.

As they passed the Imperial, Mason observed quietly, 'I'd say those are Pinkertons' men standing there on the steps. What do you fellows say?'

The others cast covert glances in the direction of the hotel and then grunted agreement. Johnny West said, 'They must be nervous, if they have to hire extra help to guard him, as well as the real law. You reckon Lincoln getting killed last year made 'em kind o' jumpy about presidents being shot and so on?'

'I'd say it's highly likely,' said Mason drily.

There were so many groups of people milling about, discussing the news that the president was going to speak to them all from the bank building, instead of them having to be squashed into the hall, that Mason and his companions did not stand out. They strolled along casually, as though time were not their deadly enemy and they had all the leisure they required to take in the sights. Johnny West said suddenly, 'What's to hinder us from fetching one of them carboys and setting it down near the bank? Wouldn't have to worry about fuses and such, I could get up on yonder roof and fire at it. I'm guessing all those high-ups will be coming together.'

Mason and the others thought this proposal over for a minute or so. It seemed to be either that or abandoning their quest entirely. With the amount of guards milling about the Imperial Hotel, it was as plain as a pikestaff that it would be pointless to try and shoot the president and his colleagues down. The odds of killing them all were slender in the extreme. Leaving the secretary of state alive would mean that authority automatically passed to him in the event of the president's sudden demise. This would not do at all, for then Edwin Stanton would, once again, be stymied. Without Stanton's succession to power, the whole 'Great Enterprise' was doomed to failure.

The civic hall lay empty and abandoned. Two hours earlier it had been humming with activity and filled with bustling men and women, eager to see that their town put on its best face for such an important visitor. Now that the president would not even be setting foot in there, there was little point in doing more. Ladders were propped against walls, where men had been hanging twisted ribbons to bedeck the place and not one person was to be found there. Frank Mason and the other five men marched straight in and made their way to the back of the stage. West said, 'You think we can set both of them side by side outside the bank?'

'That might look mighty odd,' said one of the others, 'I'm thinking that one is all we can chance. What do you say, Mason?'

'Yes, just the one. Providing that Johnson and his cronies are nearby, they'll all be killed for sure. That's forty pounds weight of explosives.' That any number of innocent men, women and children standing nigh to the president would also die was nothing to either Frank Mason or the others.

There was still two or three hours before President Johnson and his entourage were due to step through the front door of the bank and so Mason and the others faced a dilemma. Obviously, they could not start positioning heavy flasks of liquid in front of the bank while the Pinkertons' men or federal officers were sniffing around. Nor would they wish to leave the thing near the bank for too long before the arrival of the president, lest some busybody should wonder what it was. Ideally, it would be in place just before Johnson and his men fetched up there, as though it was just some feature of the street; an item awaiting collection or some such. Since the speech was to be delivered at eight, the men decided to carry the carboy out of the civic hall and put it in the space between the bank and the next building at a quarter after seven. The president's party, including it was hoped Secretary of State Seward, must walk past this place when they walked from the Imperial Hotel to the new bank, and if Johnny West could be trusted to put a ball through the container then their plans would not be frustrated.

Mason and the others went back to the Imperial for an hour or two, merely to keep off the street and out of sight of the young man who was seeking their blood. Johnny West went off to scout out the necessary position on the rooftops overlooking the bank. He also wished to get himself installed there well ahead of time. The last thing needful was for any of those guarding the president to see anybody clambering about on the buildings overlooking the president's route; especially one with a rifle in his hand! The stiller and less obtrusive he was up there, the better.

Watching from his vantage point, Clancy saw the men split up and had to choose whether to go after the larger group or to follow the man he had earlier had the run-in with. With considerable reluctance, he decided that the five men should take priority for now. There would be a reckoning with the other later. Clancy had no intention of challenging these characters yet, but wanted to catch them in the actual commission of some act of violence. He slid swiftly down the iron fire ladder at back of the building and then raced around the side, in time to see the five of them as they strolled towards the Imperial. Just as he had suspected, they turned into the entrance of the hotel. At least he now had all the rats in one trap, as you might say.

It was not hard to see that if some kind of mine was to be sprung that would be powerful enough to reduce a building to rubble then a large quantity of either black powder or nitro would be needed. There had been no sign of anything like that in the hotel rooms and so Clancy thought it might be worth checking over the civic hall, which was, after all, where everybody had thought until lately that President Johnson would be speaking. As he turned back to have a look around the hall, Clancy chanced to bump into another of the deputies, a fellow no more than five years older than he himself, who said, 'Say, you ain't seen Tom Parker on your travels, I suppose? Fellow's vanished entirely.'

'He was meant to be at the depot earlier, he didn't show though.'

'You know the Justice is wanting to speak to you? 'Bout that fire at your brother's house. Captain o' the fire crew laid an information that he had cause to suspect arson.'

The truth was that Clancy had thrown himself into hunting for the Klansmen that morning for no other reason than to blot from his mind the memory and thought of his brother and his wife and little 'uns being burned to death. He'd no wish to consider the matter now and said instead, 'I'm bound over to the hall. Might be some clue there to what's been happening. You want to come?'

'Might as well,' said the other man, a little moodily. 'Without your brother, nobody seems to know what's what any more.'

The two deputies walked down to the civic hall and poked around the place for a spell. It was the other man, whose name was Andrew Nolan, who suggested a look under the stage and Clancy mentally kicked himself for not thinking of it first. There was no illumination in the dusty and cramped space beneath the stage and barely room for a man to stand upright. The only light was that which came from the backroom of the hall. Not much entered the basement from the door that gave access. There was just about enough light though to see the sheen of some liquid on the cement floor. Nolan, who had entered first, bent down and rubbed his fingers in this and then went back to the door to get a better idea of what it was that he had touched. The crimson was beginning to turn brown, but it was clear to both young men that blood had been shed here and no more than a few hours ago. Andrew Nolan said, 'You want I should go and find the others, the deputies I mean, and bring 'em here?'

'I don't think we've time,' replied Clancy slowly. 'I reckon as things will come to a point any minute. That speech is due in a couple of hours. Let's have a look round here, see what's what.'

It didn't take long for the two of them to unearth, in the first instance, the bloody corpse of Tom Parker. Soon after that, they established by the marks on the dusty floor that two heavy objects had been dragged across the basement. These proved to be carboys full to the very brim of some grey liquid. Clancy said suddenly, 'It might be a right good idea were we to move clear of these here. I've a notion they might hold enough nitroglycerine to blow us to kingdom come.'

CHAPTER 9

Deputy Nolan might have been a few years older than Clancy, but he recognized in the other man something that he lacked, although he could not have put into words just what that might be. At all events, he looked to Clancy for guidance, saying, 'What d'you say? We wait here for them as killed Tom?'

'Yes, that's what I say. There's six of them in total. We keep our pistols out, I'd say we could surprise them when they come back for their nitro.'

'You think they will?'

'Sure of it,' said Clancy and gave a brief account of his role in getting the location of the president's speech altered. 'Stands to reason now,' he continued, 'that if they can't shoot at him without being immediately killed or arrested, then they'll have to use the stuff over there. They'll be coming for it all right.'

So it was that there began a nerve-shredding time as the two young men closed the door, leaving them sitting in the basement of the civic hall in complete darkness and waiting for a band of ruthless and determined assassins. Two hours passed in more or less complete silence, only the element of surprise would serve to give the two of them an edge over their adversaries. At length, they heard footsteps and the sound of men talking quietly among themselves. Both Clancy and Nolan braced themselves for action, cocking their pieces and training them on the entrance to their hideout.

The men hiding in the basement were at a distinct advantage when the door opened, because, of course, whereas the gang were looking into the darkness from a relatively light place, Clancy and Nolan could see the other men clearly silhouetted against the light. Clancy called, 'We're peace officers. Throw down your weapons!' Whereupon, all hell cut loose. The men of the Klan were not in the slightest degree inclined to surrender without a fight and so rather than throwing down their guns they drew them and began peering into the gloom in order to identify any target. Nolan hesitated, but for Clancy the case was plain. It was kill or be killed and so he fired twice, hitting two of the five men crowded around the entrance to the basement. This spurred on the other deputy and he too began firing at the rectangle of light, against which were outlined the men who wished to murder the president.

The Klansmen were disadvantaged by their knowledge that there was a sufficient quantity of unstable explosives down in that dark space to destroy them all. This caused them to pause before returning fire, which in such situations is apt to prove fatal. So it was now, because four of the five men were killed at once in that first round of fire from the two deputies. Mason had had the sense to dodge to one side, but was left now in the unenviable position of being alone against the Lord knew how many armed lawmen. He waited patiently, until, just as he had thought would happen, one of those in the basement, assuming that all the enemy had been killed, was incautious enough to poke his head out of the doorway and look around; whereupon Frank Mason put a ball straight through the man's forehead. His triumph on the field of battle was, however, destined to be short-lived.

Mason listened carefully for a while and then, mindful that the sound of gunfire was likely to draw unfavourable attention from strangers and busybodies, meaning that time was of the essence, and having persuaded himself that there could only have been one person in the basement all along, he walked carefully down the short flight of steps, only to be shot dead by Clancy. Now it was Clancy's turn to wait and listen. He heard nothing and concluded that it was safe now to leave his hiding place.

Leaving the basement was no easy business, so cluttered was it with corpses. He stepped over Mason and then picked his way past Nolan, who lay on his back with a surprised look on his face, staring sightlessly up at the ceiling. There were no living men to be seen and so Clancy counted up the bodies. He made it six men, one of whom was a deputy. He turned in bewilderment to look down again into the basement, wondering where the sixth of the men he was hunting might be, just as Johnny West, who had heard the gunfire from his perch up on the rooftop and knew that their whole plan must be unravelling, appeared behind him and, without bothering to aim properly, lifted his rifle and shot Brent Clancy in the back.

Clancy felt the ball strike him just below his shoulder blade and the force of it knocked him off balance and propelled him headfirst down the steps and into the basement. He was winded by the fall, but had the presence of mind to retain his grasp on the pistol, which as far as he was able to recollect, still had two shots in it. The pain in his back was ferocious, but he still managed to wriggle round, so that he was lying on his back and facing the doorway. Johnny West was a deal more cautious than the others had been, but even so he could not see very much, peering through the doorway, looking from the light into the shadows as he was. Having seen what ten gallons of nitro could wreak, he did not feel at all disposed to begin firing random shots down into the darkness. Instead, he made a sudden spring for the steps, hoping to overcome any resistance from the man he hoped that he had killed, but who might only be lying wounded.

Being injured and in pain, to say nothing of lying in such an awkward and uncomfortable position, meant that this was not the best shot of Clancy's life, but as soon as West was visible, he fired at once. It was not a mortal shot; the ball shattered the other man's right knee and since he could no longer support the weight of his body on his two legs, he too came tumbling down, coming to rest on the floor of the basement, no more than three feet from Clancy. Before he had time to catch his breath, Clancy raised his pistol, cocking it with his thumb as he did so, pointed it straight at the man's face and squeezed the trigger. He was appalled to hear the muffled click that signified a misfire. Despite the agony that his knee must have been causing him, the man gave a crooked grin and then began to use one arm to haul himself away from Clancy. He kept hold of his musket with his left hand. For his part, Clancy felt that he had done all that he could and knew that bar a miracle from heaven, this was the end of the road for him.

There was the sound of shouting and running footsteps and then they heard somebody shouting out near at hand. 'We're Pinkertons' men. Best not fool with us, now.'

The man with the shattered leg had managed to crawl on his belly over to the great, bulbous glass flasks that contained the nitro. He said, 'You've done for me, you bastard, but I'll not be taken by anybody. If I'm going, you and all them others'll come with me.' He succeeded in pressing the muzzle of his rifle against the nearest of the carboys and then smiled at Clancy. 'Adios!' he said and then pulled the trigger.

As soon as he realized what the man intended, Clancy prepared himself for the tremendous explosion that would instantly end his life and when he heard the crash of the rifle shot in the enclosed space he assumed that this was the end and closed his eyes in resignation. He opened them again when he heard agonised screaming. For a second, he wondered if he had died and been dragged down to the infernal regions, but unless hell bore an uncanny resemblance to the basement of Terra Nova's civic hall then that was unlikely. For some unknown reason, the nitroglycerine had not been detonated by the shot fired into it. But what could account for that frantic shrieking? He glanced over toward the glass containers and saw a sight that would live with him until his dying day.

Johnny West's shot had shattered only one of the carboys, but the contents had not, as he had confidently expected, blown to pieces both him, the man who had shot him and the Pinkertons' men overhead. In his final agony, perhaps West had realized the folly of depending upon the drunken sot whom he and Mason had hired to cook up the explosives. Because whether due to the lack of copious amounts of ice to cool the process or possibly because Jed Taylor had misjudged the precise proportions needed to effect the transmutation of the acids and glycerine into a high explosive, the fact was that the concentrated sulphuric and nitric acid had not combined as they should have done and both constituents had retained their dreadful, corrosive power. As soon as his shot had broken the flask, five gallons of powerful acid had engulfed West.

The addition of the glycerine had turned the liquid acids into the consistency of molasses and the sticky substance had slopped all over Johnny West's shoulders when the glass had been broken. As he tried to pull himself free and alleviate the burning pain, he only succeeded in entangling himself further in the gooey mess. Clancy had witnessed some horrible deaths in the war, but this surpassed anything he had seen on the battlefield. As he watched the man wriggling like a fly caught in treacle, he could both see and smell the flesh burning away from his bones. The nauseating stench, combined with the wound to his shoulder was enough to cause him, for the first and only time in his life, to faint.

It would be pleasant to relate that from then on, as soon as he recovered consciousness, everything was plain sailing for Brent Clancy, but real life isn't like that. His injuries amounted only to the cracking of a few ribs below his shoulder. For a few days, he was the hero of the hour, lauded and praised throughout Terra Nova. President Johnson, vastly impressed by the young man's actions, wished to award him the

Medal of Honour, but wiser counsel prevailed. Perhaps the Pinkertons' men who looked into the affair alongside the regular law had their suspicions about the true character and history of Brent Clancy, because he realized after a week or so that he was being viewed by those in authority a little more coolly. In the end, no real investigations were conducted into Clancy's background and past actions before fetching up in Terra Nova, for which that gentleman was heartily glad.

Because he had actually been sworn in as a deputy and had, when all was said and done, saved the life of the president, it was decided by the town council that if Clancy wished to stay in Terra Nova and continue in the role then that was fine with them. It was a chance for him to forget the past and settle down, which had been his desire for some while now, so that worked out to the good. When Terra Nova was granted a city charter the following year and the deputies were transformed into police officers, Clancy too became a policeman; a development that he could not have imagined in his wildest dreams at one time.

Edwin Stanton's role in the Great Enterprise was suspected, but never proved. President Johnson fired him a short while later, but was later forced to reinstate him. As for the Klan, they descended into petty bickering and achieved in the end little more than carrying out a handful of lynchings and burning a few crosses. Had the Great Enterprise succeeded, it could have changed the United States irrevocably and that it did not was largely due to the most unlikely figure in the world: Brent Clancy, one-time road agent and later deputy sheriff and police officer in Illinois.